OF HEIST
AND MEN

Books by D.A. Wilkerson

Totally 80s Mysteries

A Totally Killer Wedding
Most Likely to Kill
Of Heist and Men
A Totally 80s Christmas

Mystery Journals

Mysterious Musings
My Totally Suspect Notebook

Books by Dana Wilkerson

Throwback RomComs

More Than Pen Pals
So Much More

OF HEIST AND MEN

Totally 80s Mysteries Book 3

D.A. WILKERSON

D.A. Wilkerson
Mystery Author
danawilkerson.com

Of Heist and Men

Totally 80s Mysteries Book 3

by D.A. Wilkerson

© 2022 Dana Wilkerson

Designed in the USA

Images and fonts used under license by Canva

Published by Dana Wilkerson, LLC

Edmond, OK

danawilkerson.com

First Edition: September 2022

Paperback ISBN: 978-1-948148-34-4

eBook ISBN: 978-1-948148-35-1

Dedicated to Amanda, Emily, Jenny, Jill, Kathy, Laura Lee, Mandi, and Maura—my amazing beta readers who have helped make the first three Totally 80s Mysteries so much better than they would have been otherwise

Chapter One

Brrrring!

I picked up the phone handset on my desk. "First Community Church. This is Beckett. How can I help you?"

"Is Veronica there?" Suzanne LaHaye asked with no greeting.

"No." And I didn't intend to tell our nosy choir director where the pastor's wife was. If Veronica Coker didn't tell Suzanne she was joining the Methodist Church quilting circle, she had a good reason. "Can I give her a message for you, if I see her?"

Suzanne huffed. "No. I'll try her again later at home. I don't know why you people don't get answering machines."

We had recently gotten one at home, but I couldn't convince the church to get one. The deacons considered the machine to be too impersonal. And Veronica simply didn't want one at the parsonage. I figured she didn't want to deal with all the messages they'd undoubtedly get.

"Sorry, Suzanne. Maybe one day," I said diplomatically. "I'll talk to you later."

"Hmph." She hung up without saying goodbye.

I shrugged and put the phone back on the hook. Then, with nothing pressing to work on and nobody around to ask me to do anything for them, I sat at my desk, propped my chin in my hands, closed my eyes, and thought about Mitchell Crowe. The police detective and I were finally going on an actual date Friday night.

After four long months of him working a murder case here in Cherry Hill, Missouri—the second murder in three months in this little town—we could finally be together. Just a few minutes into our first date in June, someone was murdered in the building, and Mitchell headed up the investigation. Since I was a witness to the crime, he wouldn't let us spend time in public or alone together, though we had stolen some brief, private moments that made my cheeks burn when I thought about them.

Those moments had been few and far between, though, as he was also working another case in a town about three hours away. Mitchell was technically employed by the Jefferson City Police Department, but any time a small town with fewer resources and no trained detective needed to investigate a major crime, Mitchell was called in to help. He had an apartment in Jeff City, but I wasn't sure why, as he was rarely there.

Brrrrring!

I picked up the phone and rattled off my usual greeting, hoping the other person wanted to hold a full conversation, to give me something to do.

"Hey, Becks." My aunt Starla didn't need to identify herself. "I forgot to ask you something this morning." I lived with Aunt Star, and we usually ran into each other in the hallway or kitchen before work. "You know how Darren and I are going to the Tina Turner and Mr. Mister concert in Kansas City Saturday night? The couple who invited us had to cancel their plans last night. Would you and Mitchell want to go in their place?"

Aunt Starla had been dating Deputy Police Chief Darren Turley for about eight months, which was longer than she'd dated anyone in the twenty years since she graduated from high school. I was certain Darren was ready to pick out a ring, but as far as I knew, my aunt had no plans to get married anytime soon—if ever. She enjoyed her independence, and as the owner and broker of Hilltop Realty, she didn't need a man to provide financial support.

Normally I would jump at the chance to go to the city for a concert, but I had other plans. "I wish we could go, but the church Halloween party is Saturday night. I can't miss it."

"Shoot. I forgot about the party. Anything exciting happening downtown this morning?"

Snoring emanated from the pastor's office. "Not here at the church. Pastor Coker has fallen asleep at his desk." He always shut himself in his office to work on his sermon on Tuesday mornings, and I typically needed to wake him at some point. I glanced over at our part-time youth pastor's empty desk. "Greg is subbing at the junior high school today."

I rolled my office chair over to the window and looked out at the shops across Main Street. "Not much happening across the street, either. Nobody's on the sidewalk, and The Check is dead." The Checkered Cloth diner sat directly across the street from the church office, and I could see through the plate glass windows. "Callie's even sitting at a table reading a book." Callie Collister, one of the waitresses at The Check, was Aunt Star's lifelong best friend.

I squinted to look inside the laundromat next to The Check. "The washateria looks empty, too." I moved my gaze to the next store. "Marty's staring out the window of the hardware store at what appears to be absolutely nothing."

Marty James managed the store, and we'd become friends over the previous few months. He was peripherally involved in the two recent murder cases, and we had bonded over our joint experiences. Every few weeks we ate lunch together at The Check. Our initial conversations were mostly about the murders, but recently we'd been chatting more about life and were getting to know each other on a deeper level. Marty and I had been acquainted forever, since we both grew up in Cherry Hill, but he was a few years older than me, so we weren't friends when we were kids.

I waved exaggeratedly and caught Marty's attention. He smiled, waved back, and disappeared back into the store out of view. One person walked out of the dime store on the corner and hurried to their car. No vehicles sat at the full-service gas pumps at McCoy's 66 beyond the stoplight.

"Nope. Not much going on at all."

"Our office has been dead today, too," Aunt Star said. "No calls, no closings, no showings, nothing."

"Let's drum up some excitement. Want to meet me for lunch at The Check?"

"I do. See you at noon."

I hung up the phone and swiveled my chair side to side as I looked around the small outer office trying to find something to occupy my time. Greg's desk was completely clear except for his phone and a small stack of books. I considered attempting to clear my own desk off. As usual, it was covered with papers, books, and notebooks. A random assortment of fall and Halloween decorations camouflaged my typewriter.

I got up and moved some of the decor to the bookshelves across from Greg's desk, and I carted the rest of it to the storage closet off the fellowship hall. When I returned, Pastor Coker was still snoring, so I dropped a book on my desk in an attempt to wake him. He loudly snorted one time and fell silent.

Though I hated filing with all my being, I organized all the papers on my desk and filed them away in the cabinet across from my desk. I found an unpaid bill I needed to give to the church treasurer and stuck it in his cubbyhole.

Thinking about money reminded me I had forgotten to take the Sunday offering deposit to the bank the previous day. It was still in the safe bolted to the floor in Pastor Coker's office. However, I didn't want to bother him if he was working on his sermon rather than sleeping, so I decided to wait until he came out.

The silence was deafening, so I turned the radio on low and hummed along while Whitney sang "Saving All My Love for You."

When I finished doing every task I could possibly think of, I plopped myself back down at my desk. Before I could transition back into daydreaming mode, a car backfired and distracted me. I considered looking out the window but didn't have enough interest to do so.

My focus on the window made me wonder if the plants on the windowsill needed to be watered. As I stuck my finger into the soil of one, the squeal of tires on pavement sounded in the near distance. I looked out but didn't see any moving vehicles. Across the street, Callie stuck her head out the door of The Check and looked up and down the street. She saw me in the window, waved, and shrugged. I held my palms up in reply, and she stepped back inside.

A few minutes later, sirens interrupted my sing-along to "We Built This City." The wailing steadily increased in volume, so I went to the window again but nothing out of the ordinary was happening. Callie stepped outside the diner and peered toward the stoplight at Main and Oak Streets. She locked eyes with me and pointed across the intersection, where Cherry County Bank stood out of my line of vision. My eyes widened and my heartbeat sped up. My mother was a part-time teller at the bank, and today was one of her days to work.

I raced out of the office and through the side door of the church building. Then I took off toward the bank.

Callie called out, "Let me know what's happening!"

I raised a hand in acknowledgement and tripped over the uneven sidewalk pavement. I caught myself on a light pole, paused a moment to recover, and limped down the sidewalk a little slower. Marty ran across the street from the hardware store and joined me.

"Are you okay? I saw you trip."

"I'm fine. You know me."

He nodded. Most everyone in Cherry Hill knew about my permanent limp from falling out of a tree as a child. I often used that as an excuse for my innate clumsiness.

Two empty police cruisers were parked at odd angles in front of the bank. The lights flashed, and the doors hung open. Marty and I rushed across Oak Street and headed up the sidewalk leading to the double front doors as Officer Frank Nichols pushed through the doors and held both hands up like stop signs.

"Can't come in here. This is a crime scene."

I took a gulp of air and grabbed Marty's hand for support.

"My mom—is she ...?"

Frank's eyes filled with compassion. "She's not hurt. We should be able to tell you more soon. Stay outside, you hear?"

I nodded, and Marty squeezed my hand. Frank gave me a wary look and headed back inside. He had a valid reason to believe I wouldn't follow his instructions, as I had a habit of involving myself in police investigations. In fact, I had a knack for solving crimes before the police did. I took a step toward the door, but Marty held me back.

"Let the police do their jobs." He pulled me around to face

him and wrapped me in his arms. "You're shaking," he observed.

I nodded against his chest. "I was so scared there for a few seconds."

"I know. But Frank said your mom is okay, and we know he wouldn't lie about that. Stay right here with me." He kissed the top of my head and then moved me back to his side while keeping an arm firmly around my shoulders.

A crowd began to form around us, and a young officer, Jake Park, stationed himself outside the doors and refused to answer anyone's questions, which didn't endear him to anyone.

Edna Thorn, the local newspaper editor, marched around the crowd and stopped next to Marty and me. She eyed us speculatively before demanding of the officer, "What's happening here? The citizens have a right to know!"

Officer Park shook his head at her as I gently extricated myself from Marty's hold. Considering Edna's look, I didn't want anyone to think the two of us were a couple.

Another siren sounded in the distance, and soon an ambulance came into view. It pulled up to the curb, and two paramedics jumped out.

"Move to the side, folks," one of them called out while they pulled the stretcher out the back. The crowd parted, and the pair raced up the sidewalk and through the front doors.

"Who's hurt?" Edna took a step forward and pointed her finger at the officer. "What is going on inside that building? I demand answers!" She jabbed her finger at him a few times for emphasis.

"Ma'am, I cannot tell you."

The crowd continued to grow in both size and restlessness as the minutes ticked by. Callie joined Marty and me at the front of the pack. Thankfully the late October morning was unseasonably warm, and we weren't shivering while we waited.

Finally, the doors pushed open, and the paramedics rushed the stretcher back out. We all stepped aside and craned our necks to get a view of the person on it. Though an oxygen mask covered the man's mouth and blood stained much of his once-white button-up shirt, everyone with a good view instantly recognized him, and gasps rang out.

Chapter Two

I reached my hand out to try to touch Perry Adamson's arm, but Marty grasped my elbow and gently pulled me away from the stretcher bearing the bank's president.

Marty turned to the officer at the door. "Has he been shot?"

The crowd silenced in anticipation.

Officer Park gave a curt nod. He must have determined it was better to tell us than let us make wild speculations otherwise. Not that someone getting shot in Cherry Hill wasn't wild enough.

We all turned back to watch Mr. Adamson being loaded into the ambulance, and once the vehicle pulled away and we returned our focus to the bank, the Deputy Chief of Police stood outside the doors. A few people shouted out questions, but Darren held up a hand to quiet everyone down.

"The bank was robbed." My aunt's boyfriend was never one to beat around the bush. "As you saw," he swept his hand toward the street, "Mr. Adamson was gravely injured in the process. I don't have any other information for you at this time. If you saw or heard anything you think is pertinent, talk to Officer Park. He'll take down your information. Otherwise, please carry on with your day. If there's anything else the public needs to know, we'll make a statement on the six o'clock news."

He turned to go back inside.

"What if we have family inside?" I called out. "When do we get to see them?"

Darren turned back to the crowd and his eyes sought me out as Marty placed a comforting hand on my back. Darren's gaze softened a bit when it landed on me. "Rest assured, everyone still inside the building is fine. If you want to wait for them, I don't have a problem with it as long as you wait outside. But it may be a while before they can leave. We'll need to question all of them about what happened." He turned again.

"Did anyone try to follow the robbers?" Edna asked, notebook in hand and pen poised. "Did they catch them? Should we be worried?"

Darren spun back toward us and sighed. "When the alarm came through, we had no indication of what was happening. We—"

Callie interrupted, "I looked outside The Check seconds after I heard tires squealing, and I didn't see a thing. So they must have gone that way." Callie pointed down Oak Street in the opposite direction of the stoplight.

Darren nodded. "Thank you, Callie. Those are the kinds of details we need from anyone who saw or heard anything." He focused on Edna. "We do have one cruiser patrolling the area. There's no reason to believe anyone else is in danger right now." He turned once again, and that time we let him go.

A few seconds later, Aunt Star's candy-apple red Camaro Z28 careened into the bank's parking lot. She parked haphazardly, raced over to us, and uncharacteristically threw her arms around me. "What happened? Is your mom okay?" Mom and her much younger sister weren't particularly close, but they were extremely protective of each other.

"Frank said she's fine."

She breathed a sigh of relief. "So what happened?"

"The bank was robbed."

"And Perry's been shot," Callie added.

"No!" Aunt Star clapped a hand over her mouth.

"They took him away in an ambulance a few minutes ago," Marty explained.

"How did you know to come?" I asked her.

"Callie called me and said there was some kind of commotion over here, so I got here as fast as I could."

Aunt Star's real estate office was on the edge of Cherry Hill, where nobody could miss it when entering town on one of the state highways that crossed each other at the stoplight where we stood.

I pointed my finger down Oak Street in the direction we thought the car headed, which was also the direction of her office.

"We think the getaway car went that way. Did you hear or see anything suspicious in the few minutes before Callie called you?"

"Come to think of it, yes. A vehicle did go flying by not too long ago. I remember thinking it was going way too fast."

It must have been going excessively fast for my aunt to think that.

Edna had moseyed over to our little group, and when she heard Aunt Star's comment, she marched over to the young officer, who was talking to an elderly man and writing notes in his small pocket notebook. Edna grabbed the officer by the elbow and pulled him toward us.

"Hey! Hold on!" He jerked his arm away from her. "You just assaulted an officer of the law!"

"I didn't assault anyone, and you know it, Jake Park. You

can finish up with Elijah in a minute. Starla has something *important* to tell you." As if what the man was reporting wasn't important.

Officer Park sighed but followed Edna over to us.

"Hey, Jake," Aunt Star said.

"Ms. Beckett," he replied.

My mother had insisted on naming me her maiden name. It caused confusion sometimes at our house when it came to mail and phone calls, considering my first name was my aunt's last name.

"You can call me Starla," she said.

"I'd rather not." Probably because his boss was her boyfriend.

"Suit yourself." She shrugged.

"What do you need to tell me?" Jake held his pen ready.

"I heard a car race by the realty office not too long ago. It was headed out of town," she said.

"About what time?"

She took an educated guess, and he nodded.

"Did you see the vehicle?"

"No, but somebody else at the office may have." She gave him their names. "They should all be around the office most of today if you want to call or drop by later."

Jake thanked her and started to walk away, but Callie stopped him so she could give him her statement and get back to The Check. Then Jake excused himself to finish taking Elijah's statement, Callie headed off, and Edna drifted away from us.

"I need to sit down." I smoothed my hands down my red pencil skirt. "But I can't sit on the steps or curb in this." Then I swept my hand toward Aunt Star's form-fitting turquoise sweater dress. "Neither can you. Your dress would get snagged for sure."

"I've got you covered." Marty jogged off toward the hardware store. A minute later he was back with two brand new lawn chairs with price tags dangling from them. He unfolded the metal-framed chairs and set them on a level spot in the small patch of grass in front of the bank.

Aunt Star and I settled down to wait.

"Who's been manning the store while you're out here?" I asked Marty.

"Todd Jones started working at the store last week. He'd been working at the Dairy Queen since he graduated in May, but he wanted more consistent hours. He's done a fine job so far, but I'd better go back and make sure everything's okay. I only gave him a quick update when I ran in to get the chairs."

We said our goodbyes, and Marty sauntered off.

Aunt Star pointed at him and then at me. "What's going on here?"

My face heated. "Nothing! We're friends. We raced over here at the same time when we heard the sirens. I may have held his hand a few seconds for support."

"Then why are you blushing?" She raised an eyebrow at me.

"I'm not!"

She cocked her head.

"Okay, fine. I am. He also hugged me, but that was to keep me from rushing into the bank after Frank ordered me not to go in there."

"Did you like it?"

"What? Holding Marty's hand? Having his arms around me?"

She nodded.

I thought for a moment. "It was ... nice."

"Nice?"

"Comfortable, you know. It helped calm me down." I smiled. "Quite the opposite of when Mitchell's arms are around me."

"Be careful with him," Aunt Star nodded toward the hardware store. "I do think men and women can be friends, but it's hard. I'd say Marty has more on his mind than friendship."

I frowned. "I hope not."

Before I could think on the unsettling prospect any longer, Jake approached us and dropped down on one knee in front of me. "Miss Monahan, do you have anything to tell me about what happened here today?"

"Call me Beckett," I pleaded.

He glanced from me to Aunt Star and back again. "No thanks."

"Okay. I was in the church office all morning." I pointed across the street. "A few minutes before you guys arrived on the scene, I heard what I thought was a car backfiring, but now I'm guessing it was the gunshot. Not long after, car tires squealed. I was at the window and didn't see any cars moving. Callie came to the door of The Check, right across the street from me, and she didn't see anything either." I pointed down Oak Street. "That's why they must have gone this way, because neither of us had a view down this street. Then a couple minutes later I heard the sirens and rushed down here."

He scribbled a few notes and looked at Aunt Star. "Did you see or hear anything other than what you already told me?"

"No. I was out at the office."

"How did you know to come down here?"

"Callie called me when she saw the police cars. Since my sister works here, Callie knew I'd want to come find out what was going on."

I wasn't sure why he needed to write that down, but he did. Then he focused on me. "Do you know if Mr. James saw or heard anything? I didn't get to talk to him before he left."

"Why would I ...?" My heart rate increased when I realized Jake had seen Marty with his arm around me. Maybe he thought we were together. "Oh, we're not ... I mean ... we're friends." I didn't need him telling Mitchell what he had seen, and with this new major crime, Mitchell would undoubtedly be back in town for more than going on a date with me. I smiled at the realization.

"Ooookay. Good to know." His puzzled look told me I should have kept my mouth shut. "But do you know if he saw or heard anything? Do I need to go talk to him?" Jake nodded toward the store.

"He didn't say, but I'm certain he was inside the store when it happened. We ran down here at the same time after hearing the sirens. I'm sure if he had anything to tell you, he would have mentioned it."

Jake thanked us and walked away. While we were talking, someone had put crime scene tape across the front of the bank. Jake ducked under it and disappeared into the building.

I turned to my aunt. "Now I'm all worked up about Marty! It's going to make things weird between us."

"I think things were already weird. You just didn't notice, as usual."

Darren saved me from responding to her statement by coming out of the bank and making a beeline to us. I started to stand but he motioned for me to sit back down.

He squatted in front of me. "Your mom should be out here soon. But there's something you need to know first."

Chapter Three

"She's covered in blood ...," Darren said.

My throat constricted, and I thought I was going to be sick.

"... but she's not injured."

I heaved a sigh of relief. Although Frank had told me Mom wasn't hurt, I wouldn't fully believe it until I saw her.

"You should have led with that part!" Aunt Star poked his shoulder none too lightly.

He rubbed his arm. "You know I'm not good at this kind of thing."

"So why is she covered in blood?" I asked.

"From trying to help Mr. Adamson after the robbers left."

"Robbers? There was more than one?"

"That's your response, instead of being concerned about your mom?" My aunt shook her head.

"I am concerned about Mom! But Darren said she's fine."

"No," my aunt stated, "he said she's not hurt. But I'm guessing she's not fine, at least not mentally and emotionally. She saw her boss get shot, not to mention whatever else happened in there. Of all people, you

16

should know how it feels to be in the middle of something like this."

I slumped down in my chair. "You're right. I wasn't thinking. I just want to catch these guys!"

Darren turned my face to look at him instead of Aunt Star. "Beckett Monahan, you *will not* be solving this crime."

"Darren Turley," I mimicked, "those people shot Mr. Adamson, robbed my bank," I stole a glance at Aunt Star, "and potentially traumatized my mother. Why would I not try to figure out who did it?"

"Because I asked you not to."

"You didn't ask," I retorted. "You ordered."

"She's not wrong." My aunt glared at her boyfriend. She didn't put up with being ordered around by anyone—especially him.

"Fine," he held up both hands. "You're not going to stay out of it even if I ask, though, are you?"

"I'm not."

"Then promise me you won't do anything stupid like tracking down and confronting the robbers."

"What if I happen to stumble upon them?"

"I don't think that's likely to occur in the normal course of events."

"But what if it does?"

He sighed. "You get out of there, find the nearest phone, and call me. You don't confront them."

"What if they have a gun on me?"

A pained look came over his face. "Don't even joke about that."

"Sorry." I was held at gunpoint during the summer. It seemed all the people who loved me were more distressed by the memory than I was. "How about this? I won't do anything stupid if I can help it."

"Is that the best you can offer?"

"Yes."

"Then so be it."

Darren patted my knee, stood, and strode back into the building.

I turned to my aunt. "Your man can be frustrating sometimes."

"I won't argue with you. But he cares about you, Becks. He doesn't want you to get hurt—or worse."

She pointed at the bank door, stood, and pulled me up out of my seat. My aunt was surprisingly strong for such a tiny person. Before I could protest, I noticed Mom coming our way. I closed the distance between us and wrapped her tightly in a hug, bloody clothes and all. I started sobbing, and she patted me on the back.

"I'm okay, honey. I'm okay."

Mom hadn't called me an endearment in years—not even when I was almost killed. It was funny she was comforting me, when she was the one in the threatening situation. I finally had an idea of how my family and friends felt when I was in danger.

She pulled back from me but held on to my wrists. "I guess this means your young man will be back in town for a while, huh?" She actually grinned at me. The woman had experienced a bank robbery and shooting, yet she was thinking about my marriage prospects. She never stopped reminding me she wanted grandkids close by. My brother Rafe had two kids, but they lived in Chicago.

I laughed through my tears. "I guess he will."

She pulled me in close again for a moment.

"Are you truly okay?" This time I held her by the wrists, and Aunt Star gave her a side hug and held on. Neither of them was usually comfortable with displays of affection, so I reveled in the moment.

"I'm not hurt," Mom said, "but I think I might be in shock, and I'm worried about Perry."

"Minda!" My dad's voice bellowed across the street. He dashed over to us, grabbed Mom into a tight hug, and kissed her soundly on the lips. He had no problem displaying his affection. Normally, Mom would have swatted him away, but not today.

"Let's get you home," Dad said to her.

I asked him, "Do you have to go back to work?" He worked for the county road department.

"No way. I'm staying with your mother the rest of the day."

"You most definitely are not." She pulled away from him. "After lunch, you're going back to work and getting out of my hair."

The Mom I knew and loved was back. Not that I wouldn't love her if she were more personable, but it was disconcerting to see her acting so abnormally.

She turned her focus to me. "And you need to change out of those clothes."

I looked down. My once-yellow shirt now had pink splotches on it where the blood had transferred from Mom's clothes to my own. While I did want to change clothes, I also wanted to ask Mom about what happened.

Aunt Star narrowed her eyes at me. "Yes, fresh clothes are exactly what you need." She knew what I was thinking, and she was right. I needed to go clean up and let Mom do the same. I could talk to her later.

"I need to go to the church office to get my purse and let Pastor Coker know I'm leaving for a bit." I looked around. "Speaking of which, wouldn't you think he'd be out here, with all the commotion?" I couldn't believe Veronica hadn't appeared on the scene, either.

"Didn't you say he was asleep in his office earlier?" Aunt Star asked.

"Yes, so maybe he never did wake up. I'd better go tell him the news."

I made it across the street before I realized I left Marty's chairs behind. I turned to go back and fetch them, but Aunt Star had folded them up and was handing them to Officer Park. She spotted me and waved me on.

Wearing a clean pair of stonewashed jeans and a blue-and-green striped rugby shirt, I headed up the sidewalk of my childhood home. I rapped my knuckles on the door and let myself in. A hair dryer was running in the bathroom down the hall.

"Hello?" I walked through the empty family room into the kitchen, where Dad sat at the table reading the *Jefferson City News Tribune*. "Anything interesting happening here in mid-Missouri?" I caught the absurdity of my question and grimaced. "Other than a bank robbery, obviously. Which wouldn't be in the paper yet."

Dad peered over the top edge of the paper at me. I could see the anxiety in his eyes. He was much more of an emotional creature than Mom. "No, but it'll be in here tomorrow."

I pulled out a chair at the Formica-topped table and sat across from him. "You okay?"

He folded up the paper and set it on the table before answering. "I'm worried about your mother. You know how she doesn't talk about things that bother her. Can you get her to tell you how she's feeling?"

"I'll try. But I can't make any promises."

He nodded. "You going back to work today?"

"Pastor Coker told me to take as long as I need. I might go back this afternoon, but there's not much to do, so maybe I won't."

The hair dryer turned off, and not long after, Mom bustled into the kitchen. "What do you want for lunch, Beckett?" she asked with no preamble.

I stood. "Let me fix lunch. You sit here with Dad."

She waved me back down. "No, I need to keep busy." She opened the olive-green refrigerator and peered inside. "We've got some round steak and green beans left from last night. Will that do?"

"Sounds great. At least let me get the drinks." I stood and pulled some glasses out of the cabinet. I wasn't taking no for an answer.

I grabbed a cold can of Coke Classic for Dad, and I took the pitcher of iced sweet tea out of the fridge for Mom and me. "This fresh?"

"Yes. Made it last night."

Mom used their new microwave to warm up the food while I set the table.

As we dug into our food, I stole a glance at Dad and asked Mom, "How are you feeling about what happened?"

She stopped her loaded fork a couple inches from her mouth and looked back and forth between Dad and me. "Did he put you up to that?"

"Up to what? I want to know if you're okay."

"I'm fine," she said curtly.

"All right. Can you tell us what happened?"

She chewed her bite of food and swallowed. "Can I finish lunch first?"

"Sure."

Dad and I attempted small talk while we ate, but it fell flat. It didn't take long for us to finish eating, and I helped Mom with the dishes.

We finally settled into our usual places in the living room: Dad cocked back in his recliner, Mom in the easy chair, and me on the orange and green flowered couch they bought more than a decade earlier when I was in high school. It clashed with their new mauve carpet, but Dad declared the couch would last another decade and refused to replace it. He rarely put his foot down, and even when he did, Mom typically didn't listen. However, even she wasn't brave enough to spend that much money without Dad's agreement.

"I feel like a spectacle," my mother said. "Stop looking at me."

"Well, where are we supposed to look?" Dad demanded.

"How about you tell us what happened, so Dad can get back to work?" I knew the prospect of Dad leaving would get her talking.

"Fine. But no interruptions." She pointed at me.

I mimed zipping my mouth closed.

She began, "Marvin McCoy had just come in to make a deposit and was waiting at my teller window." Marvin was my lifelong best friend Trixie's dad and the owner of McCoy's 66 gas station across Main Street from the bank. "Suzanne LaHaye arrived a few minutes earlier, and I let her into the vault to get into her lockbox. She took her box into the little windowless room where people can open their boxes in private."

Suzanne must have headed to the bank soon after she called the church. She was one of the wealthiest people in town, so I could only imagine what was in her lockbox.

"Who else was there?" I asked.

My mother glared at me, and I zipped my mouth again, but she answered my question. "Aggie was sick today, so it was just Christine and me working the windows. She was working the drive-through and walk-up windows and playing backup for me in the lobby, and I was working my usual window. Jeff was there, too, of course." Jeff Jenkins, my former classmate and high school boyfriend, was the bank's vice-president and loan officer.

"Jeff and Perry were talking in the lobby outside their offices. Christine had been to the break room, and she stopped to chat with Perry and Jeff. I hadn't quite made it back behind the teller windows after helping Suzanne. So nobody was within reach of a silent alarm button. When does that ever happen? Never, that's when.

"Then two people came in wearing ski masks. One of them had a shotgun and waved it around. He said—I kid you not—'This is a stick up!'" She rolled her eyes. "I mean, come on, think of something a little more original. Then he said, 'Everybody put your hands up. I don't want anyone calling the cops. If I hear sirens, I'll start shooting.' The other person—"

"Was the other person a man or a woman?"

"Beckett Lee Monahan, are you going to let me tell this story or not?"

"Sorry." I pressed my lips tightly together.

Mom cleared her throat but again answered my question. "It was a woman, and she had a handgun. She spoke in a fake deep voice, and she wore a baggy black sweatsuit. She made Christine and me empty out our drawers into a green duffel bag. Thankfully Marvin was only depositing a personal check and not the gas station's cash takings, but the woman took his wallet and watch, though it can't be worth more than ten bucks." Mom shook her head, no doubt thinking the woman was silly for wasting time on Marvin's watch.

"She didn't go to the drive-through and outdoor walk-up windows, probably scared she'd be seen from the outside. She told Perry and Jeff to toss their wallets and watches on the floor. In the meantime, the guy had his gun pointed at Perry. He said if anyone hit an alarm button or moved without being told to, he would shoot Perry." Tears filled Mom's eyes, but she pressed on.

"The woman then ordered Jeff to open the vault. He took his sweet time unlocking the cage door leading into the first room with the lockboxes. The lady followed him in with her gun against his back. Then she told the man a lockbox door was open, so somebody had their box out and was probably in the room next to the vault. The man moved over there and pounded on the door.

"Suzanne didn't answer, but the guy threatened to shoot through the door, so she opened it. That caused enough of a distraction for Perry to creep into his office and hit his alarm button, but the guy caught him at it, and he ran over and shot him. Hit him below his right shoulder." She pointed to the spot on her body.

I tried not to picture the scene in my mind, but it was hard not to. My heart went out to my mom for having to witness her friend being shot. I knew how that felt.

Mom continued. "I guess they knew they needed to get out of there after that, so the woman dumped the contents of Suzanne's box into the duffel bag, and they ran out before Jeff could open the back part of the vault where the bank keeps its money. Seconds later, we heard a vehicle peel away. Christine called the police while Jeff and I ran to Perry, who had staggered out of his office before he collapsed."

Chapter Four

"That was a very detailed report." I looked at my mother with respect.

"I watch *Murder, She Wrote*, too. You're not the only person who knows anything about solving crimes."

"Hold on just a minute." Dad cranked his recliner handle and planted his feet on the floor. "Neither of you is going to solve this crime."

My mother snorted. "Ronald Monahan, after more than thirty years together, you ought to know better than to order me not to do something."

Mom and Aunt Star were cut from the same cloth when it came to men—or really anyone—telling them what to do. I was unsure how I had missed that gene, but I was becoming more confident in myself, my choices, and my opinions at my ripe old age of twenty-eight.

She continued, "I am certainly going to try to solve this case, and don't you try to stop me."

Dad flopped against the back of his chair with a huff. "You women ..."

Considering the glare Mom gave him, he was lucky he didn't finish his thought out loud.

"Between the two of us," Mom nodded at me, "plus Starla, Darren, and Mitchell, we'll get this case solved in no time."

"Who's Mitchell?" Dad asked.

"He's Beckett's young man, you nincompoop." Mom was on a roll. "Remember? The detective who came to help out with the murders? The man who saved her life out at Marty's house? Her class reunion date?"

"Why haven't I met this fellow?" Dad narrowed his eyes.

I explained about us not being able to date during the previous cases.

"Hmph. Sounds like he'll be back for this one." He pointed his head at me. "You bring him over to meet me."

"Yes, sir."

"And tell him he'd better solve this crime before you do, so you don't end up staring down the barrel of a shotgun again."

"Yes, sir."

"Stop 'yes, sir'-ing him," Mom ordered.

"Yes, ma'am." I wasn't sure how it was better for her to boss me around than for him to do so, but arguing with my mother was always a losing game.

I wanted to ask Mom more questions and start discussing possibilities for who the robbers might be, but first we needed Dad to leave.

Mom had the same idea. "All right, Ronald, time for you to get back to work."

Dad never argued when Mom bossed him around, either. With a sigh, he stood, gave Mom a peck on the lips, grabbed his keys off the hook by the front door, and turned to us. "Be careful."

That was an order Mom wasn't going to argue with. Nor was I. She nodded, I gave him a thumbs up and a cheery smile, and he left.

"We'll get this show on the road in a few minutes." Mom stood. "First I'm going to call the hospital to check on Perry."

It took her a few minutes to get through to someone who would talk to her, but Mom was nothing if not persistent, so she finally was able to talk to Perry's wife, Sandra. From Mom's end of the conversation I could hear from the other room, his prognosis didn't sound promising.

She came back in from the kitchen and plopped down on the couch next to me. "He's in surgery. He lost a lot of blood, and they're not very hopeful, but there's still a chance he could pull through." A lone tear ran down her cheek.

I grabbed her hand, and she didn't pull away. "I'm so sorry, Mom. Perry's such a kind man. I can't believe anyone would hurt him."

"I know. He's been so good to your dad and me over the years." She sniffled and then said in a strong voice, "Which is all the more reason why we need to find out who did this!"

"We will. I promise." I squeezed her hand.

"So what do we do first?"

The fact that Mom didn't already have a plan and was asking me for advice told me she wasn't as pulled together as she seemed. But annoyingly, I didn't have a plan either.

"This case is a lot different than the other two," I said. "For those, we immediately had a lot of suspects, because we figured the killer was someone who was present at the wedding or the class reunion. But for this one, the robbers came in from the outside and were in disguise, which leaves us with a lot more options."

"Well, we have to start somewhere."

"Let's start with possible motives, instead of possible suspects," I said. "But first, we need to get Aunt Star over here."

While we waited for my aunt to arrive, I started making

chocolate chip cookies. The mixer was going full strength when the faint sound of the doorbell rang out above it.

I turned around a minute later and was surprised to find a full kitchen. Aunt Star had brought Veronica Coker and Suzanne LaHaye with her. I greeted both ladies and gave Suzanne a hug.

"How did all of you end up here?" I asked.

Aunt Star swiped a fingerful of cookie dough from the bowl. "Your mom called right after I talked to Veronica, who said she was about to head over to Suzanne's. So I called her back and told her to bring Suzanne over here."

She joined the others at the kitchen table while I scooped balls of dough onto the cookie sheet and Mom poured drinks for everyone.

While they made small talk and waited for me, I wondered how the conversation would go—and how the investigation would go. Each of the four women sitting at my parents' table had a strong personality. None of them enjoyed having anyone tell them what to do or how to do it. If I wasn't careful, they'd run all over me. I made a pact with myself to be forceful with them.

I slid a sheet of cookies into the oven and set the tomato-shaped timer, but before taking my place at the table, I headed into the living room and opened the drawer in the end table by Dad's recliner. I rifled through the contents until I found a small, unused notepad. "Cherry County Bank" was emblazoned at the top, which was rather appropriate for my purposes.

I grabbed a pen from the cup beneath the phone in the kitchen and finally sat. Everyone grew quiet and looked at me, which both surprised me and boosted my confidence.

"Right. We all know why we're here. First, Mom, tell everyone what you told Dad and me. Then Suzanne, you can tell us your story."

I was under no illusions Suzanne would keep her mouth shut until it was her turn. Indeed, she interrupted Mom several times, but I intervened to keep us on track. This time, I took notes while Mom talked. Everyone even stopped talking while I took the cookies out of the oven and put another pan in.

"Okay, Suzanne, your turn. Tell us what happened from the moment you approached the bank."

"Even outside the bank?"

"Yes. The robbers could have been out there staking out the place."

"Hmm." Suzanne thought for a few seconds before beginning. "When I drove up, downtown was deserted."

I nodded, as I had noticed the same. "Did you see any cars you didn't recognize?"

"I don't think so. All the bank employees' vehicles were in the back of the lot, but no other cars were there."

"What about the church lot?" The church parking lot made an L-shape around the building, and one end was directly across the street from the bank lot. "Any cars there other than mine?"

"No."

My face dropped. I had hoped Suzanne would be able to give a description of a strange car in the vicinity, but that would be too easy.

"What happened when you went inside?" I was truly floored Suzanne was letting me ask questions instead of barreling right through her story.

"I went up to your mom's window and signed the card for my lockbox, and we went to the vault. My box is heavy, so Minda helped me carry it to the little room. I locked myself in, and not twenty seconds later, I heard someone yelling in the lobby. I went over to the door and put my ear up to it to try to hear." She moved her head to demonstrate. "It's a solid wood door, not a hollow one, but I could hear enough to figure out what was happening. I was beside myself, as there was nothing I could do to help."

Suzanne looked at Mom. "You tell Perry ...," she hesitated, "... or Jeff they need to install a phone in that room. If there'd been one, we might have saved ourselves a lot of trouble."

"That's a good idea," I said, "but I think it's probably a rare moment when none of the employees are within reach of a phone or alarm button."

"Still," she said, and Mom nodded.

The timer went off, and I switched the cookie sheets out again. As I transferred the cookies off the first sheet, I prompted Suzanne, "Then what?"

"I stayed with my ear to the door, quiet as a church mouse, hoping the police would arrive before the robbers figured out I was there. I thought surely somebody would hit the alarm or be able to slip out or *something*." Suzanne huffed, as if she'd have been able to do "something" if she wasn't trapped inside a windowless, phoneless room. Mom let her comment slide, which shocked me.

I settled back into my seat and took a sip of tea.

Suzanne continued, "Next thing I knew, somebody pounded on the door. I moved over into the corner and didn't say a word, hoping they'd think it was a locked closet. Then the man hollered, 'Open the door, or I'll shoot it open.' I didn't think twice, because it's a tiny room, and I didn't know what kind or how many guns he had. I opened the door in time to see Perry slip into his office. As you know, the man shot him. Then the woman rushed into the room with me."

"You're sure it was a woman?" I asked. "Did she say anything?"

"Didn't say a word, but I could tell it was a woman under the mask. She didn't look me in the eye. In fact, she kept her head down while she dumped all the contents of my box into her bag. I hoped it'd be too heavy for her to carry. Would've served her right, the little ..." She glanced at Veronica and didn't finish her comment. "Anyway, she dragged the bag out the door, and I didn't watch them leave."

I tapped my pen on the table with one hand and chewed the pinky nail on the other while I perused my notes. Meanwhile, Mom handed out cookies to everyone but Aunt Star. My aunt pretended she only ate healthy foods, but I knew better. Cookies mysteriously disappeared from the cookie jar during the night at our house.

Brrrrring!

Mom got up to answer the phone. She greeted the person on the other end and a few seconds later said, "I'll be there in ten minutes. ... Yeah. ... Do you need to talk to Suzanne, too? She's here. ... I'll tell her. See you soon."

To us, she unnecessarily said, "That was Darren. They have more questions for me. You, too, Suzanne, if you have time right now. The rest of you are welcome to stay here if you want."

Suzanne used the table to help push her considerable bulk out of her chair.

"One quick question for you before you go, Suzanne." I picked my pen back up. "What was in your lockbox?"

"Mostly papers—house deeds, car titles, my will, and so on. But also some rare coins Richard collected, my mama's wedding ring, and Richard's war medals." Tears filled her eyes.

Suzanne's husband was quite a bit older than her and had married her soon after his first wife died in a car accident. He passed away not long before I moved back to Cherry Hill about three years earlier. He was a lawyer and invested well, which made Suzanne wealthy—at least by Cherry Hill standards. I was surprised her lockbox didn't hold more items of value.

"I'm sorry, Suzanne." I hugged her again.

She patted me on the back. "Thank you, child. Come on, Minda. Let's get this over with."

Chapter Five

"You've been quiet," I said to Veronica.

She grabbed a cookie and sat back down at the table. "You were doing a fine job of asking questions, and I wasn't there, so I didn't have anything to add."

Aunt Star asked, "Did Minda or Suzanne say anything that struck either of you as odd?"

"Perhaps not odd," I said, "but interesting that the lady robber knew where people take their lockboxes."

"So she has a lockbox there herself?" Veronica guessed.

"Either that or they cased the place while someone was going into or out of the room with their box." I nibbled on a cookie.

"That can't happen very often, though, right?" Aunt Star tapped her finger on the tabletop. "I get into my box two or three times a year. There can't be more than 150 boxes in there, which would equal about one person getting into their lockbox a day."

"We'll ask Mom if that's accurate." I made myself a note. "We'll also ask her if anyone who doesn't have an account there has been in recently." I clicked my pen. "I might ask Jeff, too. Mom's not there every day, but he is."

"Tonight is 'Dollar Draft Night' at The Blue Barn," Aunt Star said. Our favorite local bar stood down the street from the church and bank. "Jeff will almost certainly be there tonight. Why don't we go to dinner there and see if he's around—or anyone else who might know something? You in, Veronica?"

"No. Harold doesn't like The Blue Barn. He hates how we smell like cigarette smoke when we leave. I don't know why he thinks that's different than any other restaurant in town, but he absolutely refuses to go there and doesn't want me to, either. You'll have to fill me in afterward."

"Let's talk about motive for a minute." I picked up my pen again. "Why do people rob banks?"

"I would think the answer is obvious." Veronica snorted.

"Yes, of course, because they want or need the money," I said. "But what else?"

"They have something against Perry? Or Jeff?" Aunt Star suggested.

"Maybe they got turned down for a loan, or the bank foreclosed on their mortgage." I looked at my aunt. "Do you know of any foreclosures in the area?"

"There have been several home foreclosures in Cherry County this year, plus a couple of farms. You didn't hear this from me, but I heard a rumor the Stouffer farm is about to be foreclosed on. I'm not positive it's true, though."

Randy and Cheryl Stouffer were both in my class in school. Their farm had been in his family for generations.

"But Randy bought a new truck this year," I said. "How could he afford that if they were having money trouble?"

"I have no idea," my aunt said.

"The new vehicle could be one of the causes of the money trouble," Veronica suggested.

"Do you think Jeff will tell me who might be mad about something loan related?" I asked.

"I don't know if that's legal," my aunt said, "but get a few drinks in him and he might. Plus, men have a hard time saying no to you."

"Me?" My forehead wrinkled. "Why?"

"Because you're sweet and cute and thoughtful, and every man in this town who isn't married wants to date you."

My jaw dropped. "Are you kidding me?"

"She's not wrong." Veronica bit into another cookie. I had no idea how she stayed so thin.

"But they all think it's pointless to ask you out," my aunt said, "because you turned down everybody who tried to date you when you came back to town a few years ago."

"I don't believe it. Plus, I've got Mitchell!"

Aunt Star shrugged. "Which nobody knows, because you haven't been seen in public together except those few minutes at the reunion before the murder."

Veronica gave me an assessing look. "Why didn't you date anyone when you moved back?"

"I have this problem of picking men with issues and thinking I can fix them. You know me—I always want to help. After breaking up with my fiancé and moving back here from St. Louis, I said no to everybody who asked me out. I didn't trust myself."

"What about Mitchell? Does he have issues you want to fix?" Veronica asked.

"I haven't found one yet. He's not perfect, but he's pretty great." I couldn't stop the smile that spread across my face.

"Stay away from Jeff Jenkins, though, Beck," Aunt Star said. "That would lead to nothing but trouble."

My smile disappeared. "I've already ridden that train. I have no plans to buy another ticket." I dated Jeff most of our senior year of high school. We had fun together, but we were never serious about each other, and I had zero desire to date him again. The man drank too much, and his ex-wife really did a number on him. I knew him well enough to know he almost certainly hadn't dealt with everything she put him through.

"When you talk to Jeff, make sure he knows you're dating Mitchell. But not until after you get the details you need." Aunt Star gave me a piercing look. "The same goes for Marty."

Veronica raised her eyebrows. "Marty James?"

"Yes, he's also in love with Beckett," my aunt explained.

I groaned. "He is not. Now can we stop talking about my love life and get back to the bank robbery?"

"I like Marty." Veronica nodded and tapped a fingernail twice on the tabletop. "You wouldn't go amiss on that one."

"I am not interested in Marty," I insisted. "Have you forgotten about Mitchell?"

"Not exactly," she replied, "but I haven't seen him in months."

"That's about to change."

"If you say so." Veronica checked her watch. "I need to get going. Beckett, I'll tell Harold you won't be back at work today. Let me know what you find out at The Blue Barn tonight."

"Will do."

Veronica let herself out.

"I need to do something else for a while," I said to my aunt. "Do you need to go back to the office?"

"No, let's go home. Leave a note for your mom to call us when she gets back."

When the phone rang an hour later, I thought it would be Mom, but it was Mitchell.

"Darren tracked me down to tell me about the bank robbery. Is your mom okay? Are you okay?"

"I don't think the whole thing has fully sunk in yet." I sat down at the kitchen table. "Thankfully Mom's fine. She was a little shaken up, but she'll be all right. We're both worried about Perry, though."

"Perry is the bank president, right? How's he doing?"

"Last I heard he was going into surgery. It's good to know he's still alive. It's also good for you and me that I was not a witness to this crime, and I'm not a suspect."

"How do you know you're not a suspect?" he teased.

I laughed. "I guess I don't know. But I can tell you I didn't do it."

"I was fairly certain that was the case."

"Speaking of cases, will you be helping with this one, too?"

"Darren has enough experience with major crimes now to take the lead, but I'll help out for a few days and then be on call if he needs me. The reason I called is to tell you I'll be in town for a few hours tonight to check out the crime scene and look over the details of the case. Tomorrow I'll be in court for another case, but I'll be back in Cherry Hill Thursday morning."

"Staying at The Osh?" Mitchell typically stayed at The Oak Street Hotel—known locally as The Osh—when he was in Cherry Hill on a case.

"Not tonight, but I'll be there Thursday and Friday nights, if not longer."

"Will we still be able to go out Friday evening?"

"Wild horses can't stop us."

I grinned. "Excellent."

"Will you be home tonight? Can I see you before I leave town?"

"Aunt Star and I are going to dinner at The Blue Barn

around seven o'clock. If you see one of our cars parked downtown, join us. Otherwise, come to the house."

"Great. I gotta run. I'll see you one place or the other."

Aunt Star entered the kitchen. "I take it that was Mitchell."

I told her what he said.

"If we're still at The Blue Barn when he arrives," she said, "that will be a great way to show the men of Cherry Hill you're taken. Just put a big smacker on him when he comes in."

I snatched the tea towel off the oven handle and playfully snapped it at her.

"You know you're dying to," she said.

She was right. It had been a month since Mitchell and I had seen each other in person. But I didn't necessarily want to initiate a kiss in front of my friends and neighbors.

Brrrrring!

This call was my mother. Aunt Star got on the line in her room so we could both talk to her. Mom didn't tell us much we didn't already know. The police asked her to list everyone who came into the bank before the robbery, which I found interesting. I wondered if they thought the robbers had checked to see who was working before they came in to commit the actual crime. She gave me their names to write down in my notebook. I also asked if anyone had been in the bank lately who didn't hold an account there, which she said the police didn't ask her.

"Steve Hankins came in to talk to Jeff last week," Mom said. "He doesn't have an account at the bank. I assume he came in about a loan, but I don't know any details. I don't know why he wouldn't try to borrow money from his own bank."

"Maybe his bank wouldn't give him one," I suggested.

"Could be."

"How often do people get into their lockboxes and use the room Suzanne was in during the robbery?" Aunt Star asked.

"A couple people a day get into their boxes, but it's rare for someone to remove the box and take it out of the vault. Usually people open the lid, stick something in the box or take it out, and close it right back up before I'm gone."

I scribbled down the information.

"Anything else unusual happen lately that could lead to someone being upset with the bank or someone who works there?" I asked.

"Jacqui Storm applied for a part-time teller job a couple months ago but didn't get it. Perry hired Aggie instead."

Jacqui was Suzanne's daughter who had moved back to Cherry Hill from California after a divorce about a year earlier. She'd had trouble finding and keeping a job.

"I can't believe you didn't tell me that," I said.

"It happened while you were visiting your brother, so I forgot to tell you after you got home."

My brother Rafe, his wife Cari, and their kids Jodie and Brandon lived in Chicago. I usually only got to see them at Christmas and sometimes during the summer, but I was dying to see the kids, so I used one of my two vacation weeks to drive up and visit them.

"Was the woman robber Jacqui's size?" I asked.

"Close enough, but do you think she's capable of robbing her own mother?"

"She couldn't have known Suzanne would be there," Aunt Star said.

"You can't miss Suzanne's car," I replied. She drove a white Cadillac, and it was the only one in town.

"True," Mom said. "But Suzanne hasn't helped Jacqui much financially, so maybe Jacqui is mad at her about that, and when her mother was at the bank, Jacqui didn't let it stop her."

"Wouldn't Suzanne recognize her own daughter, though? Even with the disguise, she'd recognize her walk or her mannerisms or something," Aunt Star said.

"I would know either of you two anywhere," Mom said, "no matter what you were wearing. Plus, your limp kind of gives you away, Beckett."

"So the woman probably isn't Jacqui," I said, "but let's consider for a minute it is her. Who would the man be?"

"Kyle? I've seen them out together a couple times," my aunt said. "Once at The Blue Barn and once at the bowling alley in Taylorville."

Kyle Korte was Marty's roommate and my former classmate. He still held a torch for his high school sweetheart, Marty's younger sister Karla, who was married and lived in Kansas City. But Kyle was also a huge flirt and didn't go long without a girlfriend, so I wasn't surprised he and Jacqui had gotten together, though I was surprised I didn't know about it.

"When did this start?" I asked. "And how did I not know that, either?"

"It might have been while you were out of town."

"I need to stop leaving town!"

"No, you don't," my mother lectured. "Seeing your brother's family is much more important than keeping up with Cherry Hill gossip."

"True. But anyway, I can't see Kyle robbing a bank, unless he was doing it for Karla. Definitely not for someone he only dated a few times. Now back to Steve Hankins. I can't see him holding up a bank, either. But I'll see if I can find out more from Jeff about why he was at the bank."

"From Jeff?" Mom questioned.

I told her about our evening plans, but I left out the part about Mitchell.

"Excellent plan. Your father and I will join you."

I hesitated before replying, because I wasn't ready for her and Dad to meet Mitchell quite yet.

"What?" Mom demanded. "You don't want to go to dinner with your parents?"

"I didn't say that. You caught me off guard. You're more than welcome to join us."

After we hung up, Aunt Star came back downstairs. "You'd better hope Darren keeps Mitchell busy long enough that we're home by the time he tries to find you."

I wasn't just hoping. I was praying.

Chapter Six

The next call was from my best friend, Trixie.

"How's your mom?" she said with no preamble.

"How's your dad?" I responded.

"You first."

I told her about Mom and repeated my question about her dad.

"We heard the news after third period, so I called the gas station during my lunch break. Dad was incensed the robbers shot Perry. He was upset about being robbed, too, but they didn't get much. He said to tell you to find the criminals and fast. He'll help you any way he can."

"Good to know. I'll stop by the station in the morning before work and talk to him."

"Is Mitchell coming in to help with the case?"

"Yes." I filled her in on our phone call. "I'm bummed there's finally a major crime here where I'm not a witness or a suspect, but he won't need to be here for the whole thing." I immediately realized the selfish nature of my statement. "For the record, I'm bummed there's another major crime here in general."

She laughed. "Glad to hear it. But I understand. Though when he was here before, he spent almost all his time on the cases. So even if you could've spent time together, he wouldn't have had much time to give."

"Look at you seeing the bright side!"

"Weird, right?"

"A turning of the tables for sure, but it's a good thought. Thanks."

"No problem. Tell Mitchell hello from Scott and me."

THE BLUE BARN WAS half full when Aunt Star and I arrived. I made sure we left home early enough to beat Mom and Dad there so I could pick the table. I chose a square four-top near the bar and hooked my purse over the back of a chair facing the door, so I could spot Mitchell when he arrived.

I didn't take a seat, as Jeff Jenkins and Randy Stouffer were chatting at the bar. Though I wanted to talk to both men, I didn't want to talk to them together, but I did need to acknowledge the robbery to Jeff. Aunt Star took her seat and shooed me over to them.

Both men raised their beers in greeting as I clambered up onto the stool next to Jeff. I started to slip off, and he wrapped one of his large hands around my side to catch me and center me back on the stool. His hand stayed on me a fraction longer than I felt was necessary, but I told myself he was only being helpful.

"Thanks," I said. "I'm good now."

He settled back onto his stool. "How's your mom?"

"She's fine. Well, physically fine. Might take her a while to get over the shock, though she would never admit it. And she's worried about Perry. You?"

"Still rattled by the whole ordeal, I'll admit. I drove up to the hospital in Jeff City this afternoon, but I didn't get to see Perry. I sat with Sandra for a while in the waiting room until their kids arrived." He stared into his beer. "I'm glad they both got there quickly. I don't think ...," he closed his eyes and choked out the rest of his sentence, "... Perry's going to make it."

Tears filled my eyes, and I rubbed my hand up and down his arm, hoping he wouldn't take the gesture the wrong way. "I'm sorry Jeff. I know you two are close."

Jeff started working part-time at the bank when we were in high school, and Perry hired him full-time after college. Jeff's dad passed away while he was away at school, and Perry stepped in to fill the void.

Randy patted Jeff on the back and lit a cigarette. He was never much of a talker.

I squeezed Jeff's arm and slid my hand back to my lap. He swiped his forearm across his eyes, cleared his throat, and turned his head toward me.

"Can I get you a drink?" He glanced over my shoulder at my aunt, who was pretending to look at the menu at our table, and said more loudly, "And Starla? What are you ladies drinking tonight?"

Aunt Star stepped over to join us, and we gave the bartender our orders.

Jeff turned on his stool to face me. "You planning to solve this crime?"

I shrugged. "Maybe."

"Promise me you'll be careful. These people don't care who they hurt." Jeff's eyes glistened, and he held eye contact with me until I nodded assent. I wasn't the only person held at gunpoint by a murderer a few months earlier. Jeff and Kyle were there, too. And now it had happened to Jeff again. My heart went out to him, and I lifted my hand, but Aunt Star knocked it back down to my side before he noticed.

"Jeff!" My mom's voice carried to us as she approached. "What can you tell us about Perry?"

Jeff slowly turned on his barstool and faced my mother. "It's not good, Minda."

To my utter surprise, Mom put her arms around Jeff and held him tightly. He hugged her back and squeezed his eyes shut.

When Jeff composed himself, he took a deep breath and said, "He lost a lot of blood. They said the next twenty-four hours will be crucial." He looked down at his hands. "I should have done something. I could have stopped that guy. Why didn't I stop him?" He pounded a fist on his knee.

Jeff was a large man, and if the robbers weren't armed, he could have taken both of them down with no problem. But size doesn't matter when guns are involved.

In yet another shocking turn of events, Mom put a finger under his chin and lifted it until he was looking at her. "You couldn't have done anything. If you had tried, the man would have shot Perry at point blank range and killed him for sure, and then he would have shot you. None of us did anything wrong."

Jeff's Adam's apple bobbed, and Randy put a hand on his shoulder. I blinked quickly to keep my tears at bay so I wouldn't ruin my makeup.

Mom continued, "You hear me, Jeff Jenkins. You could not have stopped this. Don't you dare blame yourself."

Jeff nodded at my mother and gave her a weak smile. "Yes, ma'am. But from now on, I'm keeping a gun in my desk."

"I won't try to talk you out of that." She patted Jeff on the knee and said briskly, "We don't want to keep you gentlemen from your night out, and I'm not used to eating so late, so we'll be off to our table."

Aunt Star and I grabbed our drinks off the bar, Dad shook Jeff's hand, and Mom herded us to our seats.

Mom leaned toward me. "I guess you didn't learn anything from him?"

"No, he was way too upset about Perry. I didn't have the heart to question him about anything."

"We can try again after we eat."

I hoped to have more pleasant things to do after we ate, but I kept my thoughts to myself.

We hashed over the details of the robbery again while we waited for our food. Dad wasn't happy with the direction the conversation was going, but he was outnumbered, so he put up with it begrudgingly at first before eventually showing more interest.

"All the potential suspects you mentioned are upstanding members of the community," he said. "What about people with a criminal history?"

"If you recall, the two murderers I caught were also upstanding members of the community," I reminded him. "But you make a good point. Who are you thinking of?"

"Well, now you're putting me on the spot. I don't want to talk badly of my friends and neighbors."

"If you want to solve a crime, you have to think or talk badly of a lot of people," Aunt Star said, "at least hypothetically."

Dad moved his jaw back and forth while he considered whether to give us any names. "All right. *Hypothetically*, what about Zane Patrick?"

My jaw dropped. "Aidan's cousin?" Aidan Patrick was the victim in the first murder I solved. Zane's dad George worked with Dad.

"He was arrested a few weeks ago on drunk and disorderly charges," Dad said. "And the police suspected him of breaking into Minnie Jensen's house last month, but they couldn't pin it on him. George didn't know what to think."

"Ronald Monahan," my mother said, "why didn't you tell me any of that?"

Dad shrugged. "It was none of your business. I didn't tell you because you gossip enough already."

Mom poked his shoulder. "I do not."

Aunt Star and I snuck a look at each other and stifled giggles. Dad raised his eyebrows at Mom but didn't contradict her.

"I didn't know Zane was a troublemaker," I said. I didn't know much about him period. We hadn't interacted until Aidan died.

"He wasn't when we were younger," Aunt Star said. My aunt and Aidan were high school sweethearts, so she knew his family well, though I didn't.

"She's right," Dad said. "But Aidan's murder really affected him. He's not been himself. He started hitting the bottle hard, and he lost his job last month because he didn't show up a few times."

"So he has a minor criminal history, and he probably needs money. He could be a suspect." I looked at Mom. "Is he a bank customer?"

"Yes. And he's the right size to be the robber guy."

"He's married, right?" I asked. "What's his wife like?"

"A little rough around the edges," Aunt Star said. "She got a part-time job at the IGA a few months ago when their youngest started school. Her name's Sheila."

I recognized the name from the nametag on the new cashier at the grocery store. "Ah, that's who Sheila at IGA is. I'd been meaning to ask."

"She's the right size for the lady at the bank today," Mom said. "Wait, let me amend that. The bank robber was no lady."

Randy Stouffer stopped at our table on his way out of the bar. "Minda, I'm sorry about what happened today. I hope Perry will be all right."

"Thanks, Randy. It's good to see you."

"Same. Gotta get back to the wife and kids." He nodded goodbye and ambled off.

The waitress brought our meals, and after eating in silence for a few minutes, I said in a low voice, "Aunt Star said she thinks the Stouffer farm is about to be foreclosed on."

Mom's eyes grew as big as saucers. "I'm learning all kinds of new things tonight."

"That's a real shame, if it's true," Dad said. "What do you think Randy will do?"

"No idea," I said. "He never wanted to be anything but a farmer."

"He's had a hard time keeping up with all the farming since his dad's heart attack. I can understand how he maybe hasn't been able to make ends meet."

"If you're thinking Randy robbed the bank," Mom jabbed her fork toward me, "you're barking up the wrong tree. While the robbers were a similar size to Randy and Cheryl, I can't see it. Cheryl works at the library on Tuesday mornings, and Randy would never shoot Perry, even to save his own skin. He knows how much Perry means to Jeff."

Mom was right. There was no way Randy and Cheryl were the culprits.

"Speaking of Jeff, he's still at the bar," Aunt Star told me, since my back was to him. "Eat up, and go talk to him again. We'll chat about something else for a while so you can finish your meal."

I polished off my cheeseburger and was about to pop the last french fry into my mouth when a familiar figure walked through the front door wearing dark gray dress pants and a white button-up shirt with the sleeves rolled up, revealing toned forearms. His eyes searched the room and locked with mine. As he strode determinedly toward me, I froze in place, with the fry halfway to my open mouth. My face heated and my heart rate skyrocketed.

"Beckett, what's wrong?" Mom turned to see what had caught my attention.

Chapter Seven

Mitchell came to a halt beside me, plucked the fry from my hand, and pushed my jaw up with a finger. Then he leaned over and covered my lips with his own. My eyes fluttered closed, and I had no desire to stop kissing him, but with my parents and likely half the bar looking on, I reluctantly pulled away after a few seconds. Mitchell popped my fry into his mouth, and as he chewed it, his gaze drifted over my face and neck, which I could feel were beet red. He swallowed and gave me a giant grin. Making me blush was one of his favorite pastimes.

As if on cue, the chorus of "You Can't Hurry Love" blared out of the jukebox.

Mitchell chuckled, turned toward the table, and held out a hand to my dad. "Mitchell Crowe."

"I sure hope so." Dad cleared his throat in a semi-threatening manner. "Seeing as how you were kissing my little girl in front of God and everybody." He stared at Mitchell for a few seconds, but Mitchell didn't flinch. Finally, Dad stood and shook his hand. "Nice to put a face to your name. Ron Monahan."

Mitchell then held his hand out to Mom with a charming smile. "And the lovely Minda Monahan, I presume?"

Mom put her hand in his and he brought it to his lips for a kiss, like she was the queen. Her face turned as red as my own, and I thought Mitchell was going to laugh out loud, but he covered it with a cough. I was amused myself, as I had rarely seen my mom blush.

Then he turned to my aunt. "Starla, good to see you again."

"And you. You made quite an entrance."

He smirked at her. "What can I say? I've been waiting a long time to be able to do that."

I scooted my chair over. "Pull up a seat."

Mitchell asked the table next to us if he could take their extra chair and squeezed it in next to mine. He slid onto the cracked, vinyl-covered seat and placed a hand on my knee under the table. I tried not to squirm and willed my blush to go away.

"You look nice," I said.

"Right back at you."

After his call, I had changed into stirrup pants and a long sweater, gathered my auburn curls into a banana clip, and touched up my makeup.

"You hungry, young man?" Dad asked. Mitchell was thirty-two—four years older than me—but to Dad, anyone under forty was young.

Mitchell squeezed my knee. "I could eat."

Dad motioned the waitress over, and she took Mitchell's order. His hand never moved.

"Did you do everything you needed to?" I asked him.

"Yes. I inspected the crime scene, and I went to the station for an hour or so."

"Were they questioning anybody?"

He shook his head. "Beckett ..."

"I know. You can't tell me."

He squeezed my knee again. "Look me in the eye."

I turned my head to him, but I kept the rest of my body still in an attempt to keep his hand where it was.

"I doubt you'll listen to me, but I can't not say this. Do not try ... no, wait, 'try' is not the word to use with you. Do not solve this crime. Do not put yourself in danger. *Do not* make me rescue you again."

"I like this man," Dad declared. "Though I am perfectly fine with him rescuing you from murderers if need be."

Mitchell and I both ignored him.

I placed my hand over Mitchell's and gave him a sober look. "I promise ... nothing of the sort."

Dad laughed in spite of himself. "Good luck trying to get any woman by the name of Beckett to follow orders." He pointed at me. "This one used to, but not anymore."

Mitchell gave me a wry smile. "I had to try."

My parents began grilling him about everything under the sun, and Aunt Star caught my eye. She pointed her head toward the restrooms. She had to know I didn't want to leave Mitchell, which meant whatever she wanted to tell me was important, so I stood.

"I need to excuse myself for a minute."

"Me, too," Aunt Star said.

When the ladies' room door swung shut behind us, she said, "Sorry to waste a few of your minutes with him, but I needed to tell you Jeff saw the kiss, and he didn't like it."

"I don't care! Jeff Jenkins doesn't get any say over who I kiss. He hasn't been my boyfriend in a very long time."

"I know. But the way he looked at you earlier—there's no doubt in my mind he has a thing for you. Don't try to talk to him again before you leave, especially with Mitchell here. He won't be open to it."

I crossed my arms and leaned against the sink. "Then how am I going to find out anything from him?"

"Leave it to me. When we're done, Mitchell can take you home, and I'll stay and try to chat with Jeff, if he's still here. That will also give you and Mitchell some time at home before I get there. In fact, I'll go over to Darren's when I leave. He probably won't be there, but I have a key. Call me after Mitchell leaves."

I hugged her. "You're the best aunt ever. I hope Jeff talks to you."

"We'll see. I doubt he'll be in the mood, what with discovering you're with Mitchell and being worried about Perry. But I'll do my best."

I could feel Jeff's eyes on me as I crossed back to our table, which made me uncomfortable. I made sure to avoid eye contact.

Mitchell's arm draped over the back of my chair, and he didn't remove it when I sat. Instead, he made circles on my back with his thumb, which kept all my nerve endings on high alert. I was also well aware Jeff could see what he was doing. Mitchell finally moved his hand when his food arrived. He ate his meal so quickly I couldn't help but stare.

"Must be hungry," Dad stated.

Mitchell looked up to discover all of us watching him. "Oh. Sorry. Force of habit. I rarely have time to enjoy my food. I usually have more important matters to tend to."

I had some more important matters I wanted him to tend to as soon as humanly possible, so I let him finish his meal in peace and engaged my family in small talk.

When Mitchell polished off the last bite of his sandwich, he turned to me. "Can I drive you home, my lady?"

I giggled and nodded. Mitchell pulled out his wallet, but my dad waved him away.

"It's on me."

The two nodded at each other in the way men do.

"Thank you, sir," Mitchell said. I knew the "sir" would bump up dad's opinion of him a few notches.

"Mitchell, it was very nice to finally meet you, after hearing about you for so long," Mom said. She had heard very little about him, but I appreciated her letting Mitchell think otherwise.

"I can say the same. It's been my absolute pleasure." He flashed her another smile.

Mom blushed again, and I turned away so she wouldn't see my grin.

Mitchell said goodbye to Aunt Star and then took my hand and guided me through the tables to the entrance. Before we stepped out into the cool night air, I turned my head and spotted Jeff glaring at us across the room. I averted my eyes as Mitchell pulled me out the door.

He held a firm grip on my hand as he strode swiftly down the sidewalk, and I had to jog to keep up with him. "Whoa there, buddy. Where's the fire?"

He stopped short and swung me around to face him. "Did you call me 'buddy'?"

"I did ...," I grinned up at him and slid my fingers around his considerable biceps, "... buddy."

"I am not your buddy."

I raised my eyebrows and moved my hands up to loop around his neck. "No?"

"Does a buddy do this?" He curled one hand around the nape of my neck and kissed me much more thoroughly than he had in the bar.

I took a few seconds to catch my breath. "Not usually."

He groaned. "We need to talk about these buddies of yours."

"Let's do that somewhere other than a sidewalk in the

middle of Cherry Hill." I took his hand and started toward his truck again.

When we reached his pickup, he unlocked and opened the passenger door for me. Then he rounded the vehicle and got in, but instead of putting his key in the ignition, he pulled me across the bench seat and kissed me again.

A sharp rap on the windshield interrupted us, and Mitchell cranked down his window. Darren, still in full uniform, peered at me and back at Mitchell. If my face wasn't already flushed, it would have been then.

"Might want to get on home," he said. "You may be able to date in public now, but this might be a little too public."

Good thing he didn't see us in the bar or on the sidewalk.

"We'll take that under advisement," I said, though I had no intention of taking his advice. "What are you doing here?"

"I was on my way home and saw Starla's car, so I decided to stop in. I haven't eaten since breakfast."

I didn't have the nerve to tell him he might find his girl-friend chatting up Jeff at the bar. "She and my parents were still at the table when we left. You should be able to catch her if you hurry." I actually had no idea how long we'd been gone.

Darren tapped his fist on the hood, said goodbye, and headed to the bar.

"Why is that place called The Blue Barn?" Mitchell asked. The bar was housed in a two-story red brick building, like the others on Main Street.

"No idea. Now are you going to take me home ... buddy?"

He lightly pinched my leg and I yelped.

"That wasn't nice!"

He stifled a smile and stuck his finger in my face. "Let me say it again: I am not your buddy."

I pushed his hand away and gave him a mock glare. "You're my buddy if I say you are."

We stared each other down for a few seconds before he

shook his head and started the truck. The radio was tuned to a country station, and the Judds were singing "Love Is Alive" at high volume. His hand shot out to turn the knob down.

I laughed. "Do you always blast the Judds as you drive?"

"It wasn't the Judds when I got here."

"Yeah, right. You have a gigantic crush on Naomi. Admit it."

He shot me a grin as he stretched his arm along the seat-back behind me to reverse out of the parking spot. "I do have a thing for redheads. But my celebrity crushes are none of your concern."

I giggled. "Just like my other buddies are none of yours."

He shook his head, shifted the vehicle into drive, and dropped his hand to my thigh. I slipped my hand around his and turned my head to study his profile.

"You stare at all your buddies like that?" he asked while looking straight ahead. The man had excellent peripheral vision.

"Only my favorite ones." I squeezed his hand. "And I only hold hands with my *most* favorite ones." Too late I remembered my hand-holding episode with Marty.

Mitchell smiled and shifted his hand to thread his fingers through mine.

The Judds gave way to "Seven Spanish Angels."

I pressed my thumb into his hand. "Wanna know a secret?"

"Always."

"Promise not to laugh."

"I pinky swear." He wiggled his little finger against mine.

"My celebrity crush is Willie Nelson."

He burst out laughing.

"Hey, you pinky swore!" I said.

"And you lied!"

"I did. Good catch. You should be a detective or something."

"I'll consider it for my next career."

He let go of my hand and curled his right arm around my shoulders, and we rode the rest of the way to the house in companionable silence. He helped me out of the truck behind him and we were halfway up the sidewalk to the front door when I stopped. However, Mitchell didn't, and with our hands locked again, I stumbled forward. He spun around and caught me under the arms before I fell.

"What's wrong?" He looked me up and down. "Why'd you stop?"

"I left my purse hanging on the back of my chair."

He closed his eyes and breathed in deeply through his nose before replying. "I'm guessing all the doors and windows are locked."

"Just like you taught me."

He sighed. "Let's go back to the bar." He grabbed my hand and tried to pull me back toward the truck, but I resisted.

"No need. Aunt Star or my parents will see my purse and bring it. Let's wait here."

He assessed the front yard. "Darren won't be too happy if we make out on your front steps in full view of all your neighbors and anyone driving by."

"I don't care what Darren thinks, but we don't need to stay out front or in your pickup. Whoever brings my purse will see the truck and come find us."

I led him around the house and into the screened-in back porch. Then I pulled him down next to me on the porch swing. When we came up for air several minutes later, my banana clip was dangling from a handful of curls. I pulled it loose and tried to put my hair in order, but Mitchell moved my hands away from it.

"I like your hair all wild and crazy." He pulled me sideways onto his lap and pushed off the floor with his feet to start the swing. "Maybe nobody found your purse."

"Somebody will eventually bring it." I snuggled into him. "I don't want to leave this spot."

"It's getting chilly out."

"I'm not cold. Are you?"

He rested his head against mine. "Nope."

The crunch of tires on gravel reached our ears, and a few seconds later a car door slammed.

Chapter Eight

"Beckett! Mitchell! Where are you?" Mom's voice carried around the house.

"Let's not tell her where we are," I whispered to Mitchell.

"She's bound to find us," he whispered back before calling out, "Back here!"

I tried to climb off his lap, but he held me tight. "You're not going anywhere."

"But—"

He cut me off. "She'll love it."

"She won't."

"I think you're wrong."

"I've known my mother for twenty-eight and a half years. You met her an hour ago. Pretty sure I know her better than you do."

"We'll see." His confidence was maddening.

The screen door squeaked open behind us.

"Look at you two lovebirds."

We both turned our heads to look at my mother. Though the porch was shrouded in darkness, there was no mistaking her beaming face. I thought I'd already reached my limit of being surprised by her words and actions for one day, but I was wrong.

"I'll just set this right here." She put my denim purse on the floor inside the door. "Beckett, call me in the morning. Mitchell, I hope to see you again soon."

I nodded, and Mitchell said, "You, too."

Mom backed out the door and hightailed it around the side of the house.

Mitchell kissed the tip of my nose. "See? I was right!"

I giggled. "That was unprecedented."

"Me being right is definitely precedented."

I poked him in the chest. "That's not what I meant."

He smiled and looped an arm under my knees. "Shall we go inside?"

I bit my lip. "I like it right here."

He gave me a searching look but didn't argue with me, which was reassuring. I needed us to slow things down, and at our current rate of escalation, heading inside would blow that plan out of the water.

Mitchell circled his arms back around me and started the swing again. "So who do you think did it?"

"Did what?" I asked innocently as I trailed my fingers up and down his chest.

He grasped my wrist and placed my hand on my leg. "Don't play coy with me. I know you already have a list of suspects in your head if not in your notebook."

I tilted my upper body away from him so I could see his face. "How do you know about my notebook?"

His lips twitched. "I know everything."

"You don't know who my suspects are," I retorted.

His laugh rumbled through me. "So you do have some!"

I rolled my eyes and leaned back against him. "Maybe."

"Care to share?"

I told him everything—Mom's story, Suzanne's story, our theories, and everyone we suspected.

When I finished, he said, "I know I once joked about you getting a job with the police, but you truly have excellent investigating and reasoning skills."

"Really?"

"I don't know why you're surprised. You've solved two murders, if I recall correctly. But I don't actually want you to work for the police. It's too dangerous."

"And what I've been doing isn't dangerous?"

"Fair point. I don't want you having anything to do with these cases, but we know that's a wish I won't be granted. Now tell me more about this Zane. Where have I heard his name before? Is he related to Aidan Patrick?"

Mitchell's comment tipped me off that the police weren't considering Zane, and I wondered if we were way off base.

"He was Aidan's cousin and one of the groomsmen who found me after I discovered Aidan's body. You probably saw his name in a police report."

"Ah. Is that where I've heard Steve's name before, too?" he said a little too nonchalantly. "Was he involved in Aidan's case?"

I shifted on his lap to look him in the eyes. "Why are you asking about Steve Hankins?"

"You're the one who mentioned his name," he said, but I could tell there was more to it. I knew he had to be tired in order to let his guard down even a little, but I wasn't going to be the one to suggest it was time for him to leave.

"I did mention him. And yes, you maybe heard his name back in March. I briefly suspected him and his son of the murder, but I don't know if the police did or not."

"What do you know about him?" He twirled one of my curls around a finger, pretending to only halfway care about my answer, but I knew better.

"He's Aunt Star's age—a few years older than Darren. Married with a son named Cory who's a senior in high school and the star on the basketball team. Steve and Aidan were best friends right up until a month or two before Aidan died, when they fell out about something. I don't know what happened."

Mitchell nodded and looked at his watch.

"You need to go?"

"In a minute." His arms tensed around me. "I saw Jeff Jenkins sitting at the bar." He had met Jeff during the previous case.

"Yes. What about him?"

"He was watching us, and he was angry. Do you know why?" How Mitchell knew Jeff was watching us was beyond me, since our backs had been to him throughout the meal.

I sighed. "You really want to know?"

"Indeed."

I held up two fingers. "Two things. First, he's torn up about Perry. The two of them are extremely close—almost like father and son. Jeff is mad at himself for not stopping the shooting, not that there was anything he could have done."

He nodded. "That's all understandable. What's number two?"

I circled a fingertip around his chest to try to distract him, and I watched my hand instead of looking him in the eye. "Aunt Star and Veronica are convinced Jeff and every other unmarried man in this town wants to date me. I thought they were exaggerating the situation, but they may be right—at least when it comes to Jeff." I chose not to mention Marty. Our friendship had been nothing but innocent, and I was determined it would stay that way.

He put his hand over mine and held it still. "You used to date him, right?"

"About a hundred years ago."

"That long?"

"More like ten."

"Nothing has happened between you two since high school?"

"Not one thing. I mean, I often chat with him when I go in the bank, but that's it."

"Good," he said. "But I don't like that you have a history with him." He removed my hand from his chest.

I frowned. "I have a history with several men, just like I'm sure you have a history with multiple women. What do you want me to do? I can't change the past."

"I know," he replied with a sigh. "I shouldn't have said that."

"Are you jealous of Jeff?"

"No."

I gave him a sharp look.

"Maybe," he amended.

I didn't break eye contact while I waited for him to elaborate.

"I guess I'm jealous he has spent a lot more time with you than I have. He knows you better than I do."

I shook my head. "No, he doesn't. Did he know me well when we were eighteen? Yes. But I'm not the same person I was then. I'm not even the same person I was a year ago." I wrapped a hand around the back of his neck. "You know much more about who I am now than he does. But even if you didn't, so what? I hate to break it to you, but there are plenty of other people who know me better than you do."

He sighed. "You're right. I'm frustrated at how slow we've had to take things."

"Me, too." I took a deep breath. "But I still don't want to rush this, even now that we can. I need us to take our time to really get to know each other. Can you do that? For me?"

Mitchell hesitated a few seconds before nodding. "I can get

on board with that, if it's what you need. I also fully understand why the entire unmarried male population of Cherry Hill wants to date you. But what I need is the answer to this question: Do you want to date any of them?"

"You really need to ask me, considering where we are right now?" I grinned and ran my fingers through his short hair.

He didn't crack a smile. "I don't know what you get up to when I'm not in town. With Jeff's attitude and all your talk about buddies, I'm not entirely sure what to think."

My heart dropped a little at the thought he didn't fully trust me. But to be fair, we hadn't talked about whether we were dating other people. I rested my hand on his cheek. "I was teasing about the buddies. I don't get up to anything with anybody—only you. I'm only dating you. There's nobody else I want to be with."

"That's exactly what I hoped to hear. I feel the same." He proved it with a kiss that left my heart pounding. "Now, can I use your restroom before I go, or are you still not going to let me into your house?"

"It's not that I don't want to let you into my house. I'm just so comfortable right here." I gave him a sly smile. "We can go in if you carry me." I loved that he was strong enough to do so.

"I would gladly carry you ... if my legs hadn't been asleep for the last ten minutes."

I scrambled off his lap, and the loss of his body heat made me shiver in the night air. "Why didn't you tell me?"

"Because I knew you didn't want to get up." He gave me a lopsided smile, and my heart skipped a beat.

He tried to stand, but his legs wouldn't work right, and he fell back onto the swing, making it sway wildly from side to side. I grabbed the swing to steady it, and he pounded his fists on his upper legs to bring the feeling back into them. He finally stood and took a few tentative steps before walking to the door with a slight limp. I dug through my purse for my keys, fumbled with the lock in the dark, and let us in. When I flipped the kitchen lights on, I blinked and shielded my eyes with my hand.

"Bathroom?" he asked.

We had a tiny guest bath under the stairs, but as it was in no way soundproof, I said, "Upstairs. You can't miss it." I hoped I hadn't left it in too much of a mess after getting ready for dinner.

Mitchell disappeared up the stairs and I filled a glass with water at the sink. I leaned against the counter and drank half of it without stopping. A minute later he thundered back downstairs, plucked the glass from my hand, gulped down the rest of the water, and set the glass on the counter.

I curled my index fingers into his belt loops and pulled him to me. Then I tilted my face up to his, but instead of kissing me he cupped my face in his hands.

"Try not to get into any trouble before I can get back here to rescue you."

"So I've got ...," I did the math in my head, "... about thirty-four hours before I can confront the robbers?"

"I would like you to never confront them. But if you insist, then yes, *at least* thirty-four hours."

"Okay, that's a promise I can make." I truly didn't want to find myself in a situation where he couldn't possibly rescue me if needed.

He kissed me in response.

When he finally made his way out to his car, I watched from the front steps as he drove away. Then I closed and locked the door and collapsed onto the couch before remembering I needed to call Aunt Star. I told myself I'd call in a few minutes, and I closed my eyes.

Brrrring!

I jerked awake with a start and dragged myself into the kitchen to answer the phone.

"Is he still there?" my aunt asked.

"He left a few minutes ago."

"Ooh, he stayed for quite a while."

I looked at the clock. "Not as long as you think. I feel asleep on the couch after he left and slept longer than I realized. Anyway, we mostly talked on the porch swing."

"You *talked?* I better not have sat alone on Darren's dingy couch for two hours for nothing."

"It wasn't for nothing."

She didn't respond for a few seconds. "I don't get all the gory details?"

"Nope. Do you ever give me details about Darren? Do I want details? I do not."

"Fair enough. All right, I'm coming home. See you in a few minutes."

I moved back to the couch to wait for her. When she arrived, she curled up on her side on the pink and blue loveseat across from me and lay her head on a throw pillow.

"Why were you alone?" I asked. "Mitchell and I saw Darren as he was heading into the bar."

"He ate and went back to the police station. He'll probably be there most of the night."

"Did he tell you anything about the case? Did you get to talk to Jeff?"

"As soon as you left, I joined Jeff at the bar, and Darren arrived several minutes later. He sat with us but didn't say anything about the case. We mostly talked about Perry."

"Has anything changed with his condition? Did Darren get any updates from the hospital?"

She shook her head.

I asked, "What did you talk to Jeff about before Darren got there?"

"I told him I knew tonight might not be the best time, but we wanted to talk to him about the robbery and possible suspects when he felt up to it. He agreed to meet us at The Check for lunch tomorrow, but he went ahead and told me he suspects Aggie Goldsby."

My eyebrows shot up. "Aggie who works at the bank? Why?"

"He was about to tell me when Darren walked up. We never got back to it. I don't know if he told the police his thoughts or not. If not, I didn't figure it was my place to force him into it tonight, so I didn't bring it up again."

"Very interesting. Did he say anything else?"

"The first thing he asked when I sat down was if you're dating Mitchell. I told him you are."

"Thank you."

"I'm glad Darren and I sat with him, though. I think he didn't want to be alone tonight, which partly explains his anger at discovering you and Mitchell are a couple."

I didn't want to think about Jeff anymore. "So Aggie Goldsby?" Aggie was new to town and had been a teller at the bank for a few months.

Aunt Star said, "Makes sense when you think about it. Your mom said she called in sick today. She also would know her way around the bank and whose keys are needed for the vault."

I wiggled down until I was lying on my back, and I stared at the ceiling as I considered the situation. "But she would also know about the silent alarms. There was no way she could predict when nobody would be within reach of one. She would assume someone would hit the alarm and know they'd only have a minute or two to get the job done and get out."

"You could still get all the money from the teller drawers in that amount of time."

"Hmm. I guess. So once she was there and saw nobody

could reach an alarm or phone, she knew they could get more —potentially much more."

She tapped her chin. "I'm surprised your mom didn't think of this."

I nodded at the ceiling. "Me, too. I bet the police did, though. She's probably at the top of their list."

"And neither of our policemen thought to mention it to us."

"Did you think they would?"

"No."

"Last time they mostly only told us stuff by accident or in order to keep us safe."

"We'll need to work our wiles on those men so they'll slip up again. I would prefer for them to not give us information for the other reason."

I turned my head toward her. "Me, too. But it'll be thirty-three hours before I can work on Mitchell again."

"No, it won't."

"He has court tomorrow." I stared at the ceiling again.

"He'll call. The man is besotted."

I grinned at her. "He is, isn't he?"

Chapter Nine

"Any news about Perry?" I asked my mom on the phone while I tried to decide between the three outfits laid out on my bed.

"No. I'm hoping Jeff can give us an update when I get to the bank this morning."

"I was wondering if the bank would be open today or not."

"The police told us they'd finish up all the crime scene work last night so we could open today. People need to be able to get to their money, and we were closed most of yesterday."

I failed to respond because I had chosen my outfit and was wriggling into a pair of red tights while trying to keep the phone to my ear.

"Beckett? What are you doing? Why did you call if you're not going to talk?"

"Sorry. I'm trying to get dressed."

"Did you enjoy your time with Mitchell last night? It sure seemed like it from my perspective."

My face heated. "I did." I didn't elaborate.

"That's all you're going to say about it?"

"Yes." I had never discussed my love life with my mom, and I wasn't about to start.

"Fine, have it your way. But don't let this one go. I like him."

"So do I!" Dad hollered in the background.

"Give me some more grandkids." Mom paused. "But maybe not yet. Try to marry him first."

"Mom, we're nowhere close to talking about marriage." That wasn't to say I didn't think about it, but I didn't know him nearly well enough yet. Until I discovered his flaws—and was sure I wouldn't try to fix them—I wasn't making any plans or rushing into anything. I'd made that mistake before.

"I'm just saying," Mom said with a huff.

"I hear you." We were on the same page about the potential sequence of events. "Hang on a minute."

I tossed the phone handset onto the bed so I could pull on my acid-washed denim skirt and slip my rainbow-striped sweater over my head. "Okay, I'm back. Aunt Star and I were talking last night, and we wondered if Aggie might be involved with the robbery." I didn't want to throw Jeff under the bus, so I left his name out of it.

She was silent for a moment. "I hadn't considered her. Tell me what you're thinking."

I laid out the reasoning behind suspecting Aggie.

"That makes sense," Mom said. "I hope it's not her, though."

"What do you know about her?"

"She's not real chatty. Friendly, but doesn't talk about her life at all. She moved here from Springfield a few months ago. Doesn't know anyone here, which is strange. Why would you move here if you didn't know anybody? Said she needed a change, and Cherry Hill seemed like as good a place as any. Anyway, she claimed she had worked at a bank in Springfield, which I think is the truth, because she knew what she was doing the minute she started. Christine didn't need to spend much time training her."

"Is she married?"

"She's mentioned a boyfriend a time or two, but I've never seen him. I don't even know his name. She just calls him 'my boyfriend.'"

"Interesting."

"You're not being very chatty today, either. What's going on with you?"

"Just tired, I guess."

"Mmhm." I could hear the grin in her voice.

"Mom."

"What?"

"Stop it. I need to finish getting ready, and I'm going to run by McCoy's and talk to Marvin before work. Call me when you know anything about Perry. And let me know if Aggie turns up for work."

"Becky! I didn't hear you pull in," Jerry McCoy said as I walked through the door of McCoy's 66 gas station. When cars pulled up to the pumps, a bell rang inside so they knew to come out and pump your gas at the full-service station.

"I parked at the church and walked over," I explained. "I'm here to talk to your brother. Is he here?"

"He's in the office. Go on back."

Marvin gave me a hug when I entered. "Thanks for coming." He cleared a pile of paperwork off a chair so I could sit. "How's your mama?"

"Yesterday she was a bit shaken up, but she's fine now. You know her."

He nodded.

"She's concerned about Perry, though," I said.

"We all are. Have you heard anything today?"

"Not yet. Mom was hoping to get an update from Jeff when she got to the bank. Now, tell me what happened yesterday."

Marvin recounted the events, and everything matched up with what Mom and Suzanne said.

I thought of something that might help identify the culprits. "Were either of the robbers wearing a ring?"

"The woman was wearing gloves." He twirled a wrench around in his hands.

"What kind?"

"Black leather," Marvin said.

"What about the man?"

"His hands were bare. Seems silly to me, but maybe he didn't think he would be touching anything. Was he wearing a ring? Let me think." Marvin set the wrench down, closed his eyes for a few seconds, and shook his head. "No, I don't believe he was."

That didn't tell me as much as if he had been wearing one, but it was something. Would a married man who usually wore a ring take it off to rob a bank? Probably not, especially if he didn't have the presence of mind to wear gloves. But not every married man wears a ring.

"What about his size?" I asked. "How tall do you think he was?"

"Couple inches taller than me. Not skinny, but not fat, either. Well built, I'd say."

The description matched Mom and Suzanne's estimation.

"Were his hands rough? Smooth? In between?"

"I'll tell ya, Becky, I'm not in the habit of inspecting men's hands."

I laughed. "Right. Anything else you can think of?"

"The woman disguised her voice, but I don't think the man did. Can't be sure, though, because he didn't say a whole lot. But if he was using his real voice, it's not one I recognized."

I stood, and so did he. "Thanks. If you think of anything else, please let me know."

Instead of waiting for Mom to call me with an update on Perry, I walked across the street to the bank.

When I entered, Aggie waved at me from her teller window, and I waved back. Mom gave me a pointed look and angled her head toward Jeff's office. Through the glass wall, I could see him sitting at his desk staring off into space. I raised my eyebrows and Mom motioned me over to her.

"What's up with him?" I asked in a low voice.

"It didn't occur to any of us that the police wouldn't clean up the blood. When I got here, Jeff was down on his hands and knees in his suit scrubbing it off the tile. My heart nearly broke at the sight, so of course I ordered him to get up, and I finished the job. But he hasn't said a word since I arrived."

I turned to look at Jeff again. He hadn't moved. My gaze shifted to Perry's office door and the closed vertical blinds on the glass wall next to it.

"There was nothing I could do about the blood on the carpet in Perry's office," Mom said when I turned back to her. "It'll need to be replaced."

"Why doesn't Jeff just go home?"

"He can't. Either he or Perry are required to be here every day. It's bank policy. They can leave for lunch, but that's it."

"Oh, that's rough. But what happens if Perry ... you know ..."

"I don't know. I guess the board will tell us what to do."

"So you don't know how Perry is today?"

"No. Why don't you go see if you can get Jeff to talk?"

"I don't think that's a good idea." Especially not after my discussion with Mitchell.

"Beckett, we've all tried." She waved her hand toward Aggie and Christine, who was working the drive-through window.

I had no doubt why Aggie failed to get him to talk.

Mom continued, "Look at the man. Somebody needs to get through to him. He might talk to you, due to your history."

Our history was what concerned me.

She read my mind. "This has nothing to do with Mitchell, if that's what you're thinking. I'm not asking you to seduce Jeff—just talk to him. You two have been friends since you were kids. He needs a friend right now. I like Mitchell, but if he can't deal with you helping a friend, he's not the man for you."

I took a deep breath and nodded. "You're right."

I closed my eyes for a moment, squared my shoulders, and crossed the lobby to Jeff's doorway. His body didn't move, but his anguished eyes met mine. My heart hurt for him. Most people wouldn't believe Jeff had a sensitive side, but I saw it a few times when we dated, so I knew it was there.

"How you doing, buddy?" I almost smiled at my choice of words, but I caught myself.

He didn't answer, but his eyes didn't leave mine. I broke eye contact long enough to close the door and drag one of the upholstered guest chairs around the desk next to him. I swiveled his leather rolling chair around until we faced each other and took one of his hands in mine, holding it below desk level so nobody outside his office could see. He looked down at our joined hands and back up at my face.

"It's just us now. Nobody can hear us. Tell me what's going on."

His face crumpled, and I jumped up to close the blinds on the window separating us from the lobby. I would have preferred to leave them open, but he needed privacy more than I needed to prove nothing was happening between us.

He sobbed into his hands, and I set a tissue box next to him. Then I stood beside him and rubbed my hand in small circles between his shoulder blades until he was all cried out.

He wiped his face and took a few shuddering breaths before leaning back in his chair.

Then he turned to me and touched my arm. "You have no idea how much I want to kiss you right now." His eyes were still full of pain, not desire, so his declaration didn't disarm me as much as it could have.

I removed his hand and gently placed it on the arm of his chair. "You think you do, but what you really want is comfort. I'll give you what I can, but you know I have a boyfriend, and I know you're not that kind of guy." I wasn't one hundred percent sure of the last part, but I felt it needed to be said.

He groaned and dropped his head into his hands again. "I'm so sorry. I shouldn't have said that. You're being kind to me because you simply can't help it, and I'm being a complete jerk in return."

"You said what you felt, which isn't necessarily a bad thing, but you're not thinking straight right now. And I'm not being kind only because I can't help it. I do care about you, but not in that way."

He looked up at me with glistening eyes. "Forgive me?"

"Of course."

"Will ... your boyfriend forgive me?"

"I don't think he needs to know. Like I said, you weren't thinking straight. There's no reason to make a big deal out of it. We'll forget it ever happened."

Jeff nodded and I dropped back down into my chair.

"Talk to me. You can't keep it all bottled up inside."

He clenched his fists and took a deep breath. I sat silently while he considered what to share.

"I didn't cry when my dad died."

I didn't expect the conversation to take that turn. "No?"

"No. I wasn't sad. I was angry."

"I get that." Jeff's dad had gotten drunk and wrapped his

truck around a tree on his way home from the bar. Thankfully nobody else was in the truck, and no other cars were involved.

"But now I'm sad *and* angry. I can't believe I'm about to lose Perry, too."

"We don't know that for sure." I hesitated, because maybe Jeff did know. "Do we?"

He shook his head. "Sandra called me early this morning. Said he's the same."

"Stable is good, isn't it? At least he's not worse."

"I don't know. I just can't believe it happened."

Jeff didn't say anything else, so I prompted him. "Tell me about this morning when you got here."

He looked down at his hands. "I can't," he whispered.

"You need to, and who else are you going to tell? Kyle?"

He laughed, which made me smile. If he could laugh, he could get through this.

"Kyle would tell the world," he said.

"He would. But I promise I won't tell a soul."

He looked me in the eye. "I know you won't."

I sometimes had trouble keeping my mouth shut, but I didn't share my friends' secrets with anyone.

"Come on. Tell me."

He opened his mouth, but nothing came out. He dropped his head and closed his eyes.

"If I hold your hand, will you not take it the wrong way?"

He answered by holding his hand out to me. I gripped it gently, and he wrapped his fingers around mine, but he didn't open his eyes. He took a few deep breaths, and I rested our hands on his knee. I couldn't help but think back to my flippant comment to Mitchell about holding hands with my buddies. This felt nothing like holding Mitchell's hand, though.

Jeff cut into my wandering thoughts. "I made sure to get here before anyone else. I knew it was going to be hard. Like always, I came in the back door." He sucked in some more breaths, and I tightened my hold on his hand. "I walked up the hall into the lobby and turned the lights on, and that's when I saw it." He squeezed my hand so tightly I thought he would cut off the circulation.

"What did you see?"

He didn't respond, and while I waited for him to answer, my hand started to go numb. I flexed my fingers, and he loosened his grip.

"Jeff, look at me."

When he lifted his head and opened his eyes, I knew I couldn't make him say it.

"You saw the blood."

He nodded.

"And you cleaned it up."

He nodded, and his eyes filled with tears again. I felt a hot burst of anger at Darren. He sat with Jeff at the bar, knowing how upset he was, but didn't tell him somebody would need to clean up the mess. He could have at least told my mom, if he thought Jeff couldn't handle it. The man would be getting an irate phone call from me in the near future. Mitchell wasn't off the hook, either.

"I couldn't leave it there for the women to see. I didn't want them to go through that."

"But then my mom came in."

"I hate myself for being relieved she insisted on finishing the job."

"She was glad to do it. Mom knows how hard this is for you."

Jeff squeezed my hand. "I could maybe have handled this better if the last couple of years hadn't been so rough. All that stuff with Donna …," he trailed off.

While I figured he needed to get some things off his chest about his ex-wife, now was not the time, and I wasn't the best person for him to talk to about her. "You've been through a lot. It would probably help if you talked to somebody about all of it." At his hopeful look, I continued, "But not me." I gently pulled my hand out of his grasp.

He sighed.

"Maybe Marty?" I suggested. "I know you two aren't close, and it might be a little weird at first, but he's great at talking things through. He helped me deal with everything that happened this summer."

"Oh, yeah?" Jeff raised a questioning eyebrow.

"Not like that." I flicked his knee. "Get your mind out of the gutter. Anyway, I can ask Marty if he'd be willing to talk with you."

"No, don't do that," he said quickly. "But I'll think about it."

"Good."

"Thanks for coming in here and, well, being you. I'm still sad—and mad—but it doesn't seem quite as terrible now."

"I'm glad I could help."

"And I truly am sorry about ..."

"I don't know what you're talking about." I grinned at him, and he gave me a slight smile in return. "We still on for lunch? Or do you want to talk about it now?"

"I don't want to do it here, so I'll see you and Starla at noon."

He moved my chair back around the desk and reached for the doorknob but didn't grasp it. "Are my eyes red? Do I look like I've been crying? I have a reputation to uphold, you know." He gave me a genuine smile.

I chuckled. "Wouldn't want you to ruin your rep. They're a little red. After I leave, go to the bathroom, and wash your face and eyes with cold water."

"Thanks again. Truly."

He put his hand on the doorknob, but I covered it with mine before he could turn it. He gave me a confused look.

"One more thing." I hesitated. "Losing yourself in the bottle won't help."

He hung his head. "I know."

"If you get too low in these next few days, instead of cracking open a beer, call me. Call Randy. Call anyone. Well, maybe not Kyle."

He laughed. Before I could consider whether I might regret it, I hugged him.

Chapter Ten

J eff wrapped his arms around me for only a few seconds before letting go. Then he opened his office door, and I slipped out. He didn't shut the door behind me, but he left the blinds closed.

Mom crooked her finger at me, and I headed back over to her window. Christine was with a customer, but Aggie watched me speculatively as I crossed the lobby.

"How'd it go?" Mom whispered.

"He'll be okay," I said in a low voice.

"Did he say how Perry is?" she asked at normal volume.

"He's the same. I'm choosing to believe that's good news."

I cut my eyes to Aggie as soon as I got the words out, and she let out a burst of air, as if she'd been holding her breath. I wasn't sure how to take her response. I didn't think she'd been around long enough to form a close bond with Perry. Not that any normal person would want their boss to die, but there was something a little off about her response, especially if she hadn't witnessed the shooting.

"You feeling better today, Aggie?" I asked.

"Uh, yeah," she stammered. "I'm fine. I mean, I'm upset about what happened here, though. So terrible."

"Yeah, especially for Perry."

"Uh-huh. I can't believe it."

"Neither can I."

My eye caught the clock on the wall behind her. "Whoops. I'm late for work. I gotta run." I turned to Mom. "Call me if you get any news about Perry."

When I entered the church office, Pastor Coker, Veronica, and Greg were talking to each other animatedly.

"There you are!" Veronica threw her arms around me, which was bewildering, as she wasn't a hugger. "Your car is outside, but we couldn't find you anywhere. Don't scare us like that."

"Sorry," I said when she pulled away. "I dropped into the bank to see if they had any news about Perry, and time got away from me."

Veronica gave herself a small shake, as if getting back into her normal brusque mode. "Next time, leave a note or something."

"I'll keep that in mind."

"What did you hear about Perry?" she demanded.

"He's the same."

"I'm planning to head over to Jeff City this afternoon to see him," Pastor Coker said. The Adamsons weren't members at First Comm, but Perry and the pastor had become friends over the ten years the Cokers had been in town.

"I'm glad. Sandra will appreciate it, even if Perry doesn't realize you're there." I turned to Veronica. "What are you doing here?"

"I wanted to talk to you about ... the pantry."

"The pantry?"

"Yes, it's a mess. We need to get it organized."

The pantry was one hundred percent organized.

"Let's go take care of it." She took me by the hand and dragged me out of the office.

When the door shut, I pulled my hand out of hers. "What is happening here?"

She marched down the hallway, and I hurried to catch up.

"I needed to get you out of there to talk to you, and that was the first thing to pop into my head."

"The pantry?"

"Yes. Now, come on. We need to actually go to the pantry, in case Harold comes looking for us."

I trailed her to the kitchen. She motioned for me to follow her into the pantry and closed the door behind us.

"Don't want anyone overhearing us."

"Anyone ... like your husband?"

"Yes. You know he doesn't like me getting involved in these investigations."

She tested the sturdiness of a large cardboard box in the corner of the small room and sat on it. "I hear your detective came to town last night."

I could feel the heat moving from my chest to my face. "Where did you hear that?"

"Georgia was at The Blue Barn."

"Ah." Georgia Olean was one of Veronica's closest friends and a member at First Comm.

"He made quite an impression."

I covered my face with my hands. "Oh, no."

"Oh, yes. She thought it was romantic."

I peeked through my fingers at her. "That's one word for it."

She touched my arm. "It's a good word. There's nothing to be ashamed of. He likes you, and he doesn't care who knows it. I appreciate that in a man."

I lowered my hands. "I like that perspective. Thank you."

"You're welcome. Now, tell me what you've found out, and I'll tell you what I learned."

"Ooh, you learned something?"

"Yes, but you first. Pull up a box and get comfy."

I dragged a box out from under a shelf and sat. Then I told her everything I had discovered since we last spoke. I mentioned Aggie, but I didn't connect the idea to Jeff. If he was wrong, nobody else needed to know he suspected his co-worker. I also didn't tell Veronica about the bank not being clean when Jeff arrived, as it wasn't directly related to the investigation.

"I don't know much about this Aggie," she said.

"Nobody really does, from what Mom says."

"Seems suspicious to me."

"Exactly."

"Is there anyone else at the bank who could be involved? Were any other part-time employees not scheduled to work yesterday? Or what about an employee who was there but could have tipped the robbers off about what to do? What about Jeff Jenkins?"

"No!"

Veronica's eyes opened wide.

"Sorry," I said. "It wasn't him. I promise you, Jeff had nothing to do with this."

"You're sure?" She narrowed her eyes at me.

"Positive," I said vehemently. "Perry is like a father to him."

"All right. No need to bite my head off. We also know your mom had nothing to do with it. What about Christine?"

"She has worked at the bank forever. Literally as long as I can remember. She and her husband aren't hard up for money. He's retired with a good pension, and she works to give herself something to do, not because she has to. I can't see it."

"Was anyone else not working?"

"Frances Coolidge works on the days Mom is off. She's not the right size to be the woman robber, though."

"No, I wouldn't think so. No other part-timers?"

"Only a couple of high school and college kids in the summertime."

"Who?"

"Peter Young and Kimberly Banner worked there this summer."

"Coach Banner's daughter?"

Coach Banner had been the varsity boys' basketball coach and high school P.E. teacher since I was in junior high. His daughter graduated from high school in the spring and attended the University of Missouri in Columbia.

"Yes," I confirmed. "She goes to school at Mizzou now."

"I saw her yesterday morning."

"You did not!"

Veronica gave me a perturbed look. "I did. When I was on my way to the Methodist Church for the quilting circle, I met a car I didn't recognize, so of course I looked to see who was in it. A man was driving, though he wore a cap pulled down so low I couldn't see his face. But I'm positive the Banner girl was in the passenger seat."

"On a Tuesday morning, I would think she'd be in class."

"You would think so, but she wasn't."

"What kind of car was it?"

"A blue two-door something. Maybe a Chevy."

"We need to tell the police."

"You want me to call them?" Veronica asked.

"I need to call Darren anyway, so I'll let him know." I shifted on my box. "Now tell me what you learned."

"Georgia told me Steve Hankins banks at County Savings and Loan. Several weeks ago she saw him storming out of the loan officer's office. You know how mild-mannered that man usually is, so she was shocked."

"Yeah, but if he was going to rob a bank, wouldn't he rob his instead of ours? I don't think it could be him."

"That's a good point. You mentioned Jacqui Storm. She has gone out with Kyle a few times, like you said, but she is also dating a man from Taylorville who is nothing but trouble, according to Suzanne."

I was slowly sinking into the box, so I stood. "Now that is interesting. Do you know his name?"

"His first name is Sam. Don't know his last."

"I don't know if I should tell the police about him or not."

"Up to you." Veronica stood as well. "Let's get out of here. It's getting stuffy."

The phone started ringing the moment we stepped back into the kitchen. I picked it up in time to hear Greg greeting the caller via his office extension.

"Hi, Greg. Is Beckett there?" Mitchell asked.

"I'm here!" I said.

"Oh, hi," Greg said. "I'll hang up now." The line clicked.

Veronica waved and disappeared into the hall.

I leaned a hip against the kitchen counter. "Hey there."

"Hi, beautiful."

I smiled and my face reddened.

"You're blushing, aren't you?" he asked.

"Yes. I thought you were in court."

"I'm on a pay phone in the courthouse during a short recess."

"Did you have something to tell me?"

"I mostly wanted to hear your voice, but I need to tell you one thing. You can mark both Kyle Korte and Zane Patrick off your suspect list."

"Oh?"

"I stopped for gas at the Quick Mart on my way out of town last night, and Kyle was filling up his Jeep. Said he was getting back home from a hunting trip to South Dakota with

Zane and a few other guys. No reason not to believe him, as it could be easily verified."

"I didn't really think Kyle had anything to do with it, but it's good to know for sure. Why would they go all the way to South Dakota to hunt?"

"No idea. They're calling us back in, so I gotta run. I'll talk to you later."

I barely got my goodbye out before he hung up. I wished I had gotten a chance to tell him about Jacqui's boyfriend, as the talk about Kyle had given me an excellent opening. I also didn't get to talk to him about the mess in the bank. That was a conversation I wasn't looking forward to, though, so I wasn't upset about not getting the chance. I did, however, want to yell at Darren about it, so I hung up and called the police station. I knew the number by heart after having to use it so much over the past seven months.

"Cherry Hill Police. Barbara speaking."

"Hi, it's Beckett. Is Darren in?"

"Hey, Becky. He's here. Let me see if he's busy."

I waited while she put me on hold.

"He said he can call you in about ten minutes," she said. "You at the church?"

"Yep. Thanks."

As I headed back to the office, I realized I couldn't talk to Darren in the presence of Greg and Pastor Coker, and I didn't want them to accidentally pick up the phone while I talked to him from the kitchen extension, so I decided to go to the police station.

"Who was on the phone?" Greg asked when I entered the room.

"Mitchell Crowe."

"Oh." I was keenly aware Greg was one of the men in Cherry Hill who wanted to date me, because he had asked me out several times earlier in the year. I had turned him down each time, and he was gracious about it, but I knew he was still interested in me. Therefore, he was not Mitchell's biggest fan. What Greg didn't realize was I had no desire to date him even if Mitchell weren't on the scene. Greg was a nice guy, but he was immature, and I wasn't attracted to him.

I decided it was best to be blunt. "He was here last night to see the crime scene, and he'll be back tomorrow to help out with the case. It's nice we can officially date now that I'm not a suspect or witness in the crime he's investigating."

Greg nodded and gave me a shaky smile.

"Anyway," I said, "I need to run an errand. I should be back in twenty minutes or so."

"I'll hold down the fort."

"Thanks." I grabbed my purse and headed out the door.

Barbara raised her eyebrows at me when I entered the wood-paneled lobby of the police station.

"I decided it would be easier to come talk to him here," I explained.

She nodded and disappeared into "the pit," a large, open area where all the officers' desks were located. I sat in one of the cold metal folding chairs and picked up an old issue of *Redbook* from the small table next to me.

"You can go on back." Barbara resumed her seat behind the desk.

I threaded my way through the desks and entered Darren's office at the rear of the room. I closed the door behind me but didn't take a seat. I wanted to feel like I had the upper hand by being taller than Darren, though even with him sitting, I didn't have many inches on his six-foot, five-inch frame.

"What's up?"

I jabbed my pointer finger toward him and tried to keep my voice at a normal volume, but it increased as I went along. "What's up is this morning Jeff Jenkins had to clean Perry Adamson's blood off the floor of the bank, because nobody thought to tell him the police aren't responsible for the cleanup."

Darren blew out a hard breath and had the grace to look ashamed. "Oh."

"'Oh,' is right. You even saw the man last night and didn't mention it."

He linked his hands behind his head and looked at the ceiling. "I'm so sorry. That had to be terrible for him."

"It was. And you need to apologize to him, not me."

He looked me in the eye. "I will."

"And to my mom, because she finished the job."

"Yes, ma'am."

"Thank you."

"You want to sit down now? Or do you need to yell at me about something else first?"

I plopped down into the chair across from him. "That's the only thing I'm mad at you about. For now."

He chuckled. "You sure?"

"Now that you mention it," I jabbed my finger at him again, "stop telling Mitchell and me when and where we can kiss. It's a free country, you know."

"I do know. I've helped keep it free. I just don't want you to be fodder for gossip."

"I appreciate the sentiment, but we're adults. I can promise you we're not going to make a spectacle of ourselves every time we're together in public. But even if we do, it's none of your business."

"Got it." He placed his hands flat on his desk. "Anything else you need to get off your chest?"

I stuck my pinky nail between my teeth and thought for a moment. "No."

"Can I get back to my investigation now?"

I held up a finger. "I can help you with that."

Chapter Eleven

Darren sighed, tilted his chair back, and gave me an exasperated look. "Can you, now?"

"Don't look at me like that."

"Like what?"

"Like I'm a silly woman who can't possibly have anything productive to add to your investigation."

He removed all expression from his face. "Is this better?"

"A little. But now you look bored."

"Trust me, I am anything but. And I don't think you're silly. You have solid detective skills, but you know how I feel about you getting involved in these investigations. I don't ever want to visit you in the hospital because of it." He clenched his jaw. "Or worse, the morgue."

"I'm glad you care about my wellbeing, but again, I'm an adult. For what it's worth, I did promise Mitchell I wouldn't confront the robbers until he's back in town."

He gave me a wry smile. "How considerate of you."

"I thought so."

"Out with it, then. What do I need to know?" He held up a

hand. "Wait. Detective Crowe filled me in on your thoughts from last night. Tell me only what you've learned today."

I told him about Kimberly Banner, and he scribbled notes as I spoke. "I don't know what her motive would be, though."

He nodded but didn't theorize. "I'll need to talk to Mrs. Coker directly about this car she saw."

"I'll tell her to call you."

I picked up a Rubik's Cube from his desk and twirled the top layer around. "By the way, did anybody at Hilltop Realty see the car Aunt Star heard zooming past yesterday around the time of the robbery?"

Darren simply looked at me.

"If you're not going to tell me, I'll go over there and ask everyone myself."

"I can't believe you didn't already or that Starla didn't tell you." He nodded toward my hands. "Put that down. You're messing it up."

I gingerly placed the cube back where I'd found it. "Sorry. I didn't realize you'd be touchy about it."

"I'm not touchy."

"No?"

He shrugged.

"Well?" I asked. "You going to tell me about the car?"

"Somebody did see the car speed by. They think it was a two-door light blue or green car."

"Aha!" I thrust a finger into the air. "Like the one Kimberly Banner was riding in."

"Many cars in the area answer that description. Now, is there anything else? I need to get back to work."

"This isn't work?" I raised my eyebrows. "I'm giving you clues."

"We like to call them leads."

"Okay, I'm giving you leads."

"I guess I can't argue with you on that."

"Last thing: What are your thoughts on Aggie Goldsby as a suspect?"

He tapped his pen on his desk and narrowed his eyes at me. "What are your thoughts on Aggie?"

I laid out my case against her. Since Darren didn't take many notes, I assumed I wasn't telling him much he hadn't already considered.

"Those are some excellent deductions. Anything else?"

"One more last thing. Jacqui Storm is dating some guy from Taylorville named Sam. Suzanne's not a fan."

"She's not a fan of many people," he said, but he wrote the name down anyway.

"True. Oh, here's a final last thing. Veronica said Georgia Olean said Steve Hankins stormed out of a meeting with the loan officer at County Savings and Loan a few weeks ago."

He scribbled in his notebook. "Any more last things?"

I stood. "Nope. That's it." I opened the door. "I'll tell Veronica to call you."

"And I'll call Jeff and your mom."

"Thanks."

"Want me to report in afterward?" He smirked at me.

I rolled my eyes and walked away.

"Is there a reason you two are sitting on the same side of the booth?" Callie put one hand on her hip and used her order pad to point back and forth between Aunt Star and me.

"Jeff is joining us," Aunt Star said.

"Jeff Jenkins? Why?"

Giant hands clasped Callie's shoulders and moved her to the side, and Jeff slid in across from us. "None of your beeswax." He winked at her.

"I see how it is." Callie playfully swatted his shoulder. "What are you drinking?"

We gave her our drink orders and she scooted off. I wanted to ask Jeff if Darren called him, but since Aunt Star didn't know about that situation, I decided not to bring it up.

"Tell us everything," I said, "starting from the time you arrived at the bank yesterday morning."

Unfortunately, his story didn't reveal any information we didn't already know.

"What can you remember about the woman—height, eye color, mannerisms, anything?"

"She was about your size." He nodded toward Aunt Star, who was of similar size to Aggie, Jacqui, and Kimberly. "I didn't get a good look at her eyes." He pursed his lips. "One thing I did notice is she ran her hand down the side of her head two different times. I thought it was a funny movement, but now that I think about it, it's like women do when they tuck their long hair behind their ears." He demonstrated the movement on his own head.

"So she was subconsciously doing it." I tucked my own curls behind my left ear. "Which means she has long hair."

"Aggie has long hair," Jeff said quietly so he wouldn't be overheard by other diners.

"So do I, so does Jacqui, and so does Kimberly Banner— or at least she did this summer." I made a mental note to ask Veronica if she still did. "A lot of women have long hair."

"Yeah, but some of them wear those little metal clip things to hold it back," Jeff said.

"You mean a barrette?"

"Sorry I'm not up on the terminology for women's hair ... things."

I laughed.

"If they wear a clip—barrette—" he gave me a pointed

look, "they probably don't try to push their hair behind their ears, right?"

"Probably not."

"Hold up," Aunt Star said to me, "why did you mention Kimberly Banner?"

Callie appeared with our plates. "What's this about Kimberly?"

Jeff gave her a wary look.

"Callie helps us with all our investigations," I told him. "We can trust her."

Callie turned to survey her other tables for a moment and then nudged Jeff over so she could sit. "Everybody's taken care of for the moment, so spill. Quickly."

I told her what we knew about Kimberly.

Jeff gave a low whistle. "Man, I thought for sure it was Aggie, but maybe not. I don't know what Kimberly's motive would be, though."

Callie twisted in her seat so she could look Jeff in the eye. "You suspect Aggie? From the bank?"

"I do."

I told Callie what I knew about Aggie. "Jeff, what else do we need to know?"

"She's real secretive. There's a boyfriend, but she never says his name and we've never seen him. And a few times, when I called her name, she didn't respond. It's odd. She has also never called in sick before. Not that people aren't allowed to get sick, but it's not a habit for her." He shook his head. "She's been late a couple times recently, but only by a few minutes, so we've let it slide because overall she's a great employee. But something about her lately seems a little off. I can't put my finger on it."

Callie stood. "I need to take care of my other tables. I'll let you know if I hear anything useful."

I took a few bites of my meal as I organized my thoughts.

"Do you have any other suspects?" Jeff asked.

"Yes, Jacqui Storm." I told him what we knew.

"You really think she would rob her own mother?"

"That's the main issue with her being a suspect," Aunt Star said. "It's hard to believe she's capable of it."

I pointed a fry at Jeff. "Did you tell the police your suspicions about Aggie?"

"No. I didn't start thinking about her until after they questioned me. And I'm not sure if I should say anything to them anyway. If it's not her, I don't want her to know I suspected her."

"But if it is her, you need to tell them what you know."

Jeff sighed.

"What if we tell Darren he should ask you about Aggie?" I asked Jeff. "Then it wouldn't be you going to the police, but them asking you about her. I'm confident she's already an official suspect."

Jeff wolfed down his last bite of chicken fried steak. "I like that plan. If the cops ask me questions, I'm supposed to answer them honestly, right?"

"Yes."

"Okay. I'll talk to him. It makes me nervous Aggie is at the bank today. Speaking of the bank, I need to get back." He stood. "Tell Darren I can stop by after we close today, if that works for him. Oh, and lunch is on me."

"You don't need to—"

"I know," he interrupted me, "but I want to. I owe you big time."

As he headed to the cash register to pay, Aunt Star whispered, "Why does he owe you?"

"Can't tell you," I whispered back. "Don't try to make me."

Her eyes widened. "He didn't ...?"

"Don't even go there. I helped him out a bit this morning, that's all. Leave it."

"Ooookay. Now, are we going to keep sitting here on the same side of the booth like a couple of weirdos, or are you going to move?"

I slid my nearly empty plate to the other side of the table and moved across from my aunt. "Happy now?"

"Exceedingly." She checked her watch. "I need to leave in a few minutes. Anything else you need to tell me that you couldn't tell Jeff?"

I told her what I learned from my conversations with Veronica and Darren.

"Why did you go see Darren?"

Whoops. I couldn't tell her the real reason. But I also wouldn't lie to her.

"I wanted to tell him about Kimberly Banner."

"Why didn't you call? Or send Veronica?"

"I didn't want anyone at church to hear me talking to him. And I didn't tell Veronica to call him because I wanted to see if I could pry any information out of him while I was there. Turned out he needed to talk to her anyway, but I did learn a few things from him. Why don't you call him about talking to Jeff and see if you can sweet talk anything out of him while you're at it?"

"Oh, I'll work my charms on him. They'll be more effective if I stop by instead of call." She wiggled her eyebrows at me and I rolled my eyes, but I knew she was right.

A few minutes later, we headed toward the door, but a church member stopped me to ask about the Halloween party, so Aunt Star left without me. When I stepped outside a few minutes later, I decided to check in with Marty before heading back to work. I hadn't talked to him since he left me outside the bank after the robbery, and I wondered if he had any information to add to my notebook.

A bell dinged when I entered the hardware store, and the smell of paint reminded me I wanted to paint my bedroom to match one of the colors in my new Laura Ashley bedspread.

Todd's head popped up over a shelf to my left. "Hello. Can I help you find anything?"

"Is Marty here?"

"Up here!" Marty called from above.

I looked up the stairs in front of me to the second floor where they stocked the toys and sports equipment. Marty waved me up. When I was near the top, I looked up at him instead of at the stairs, and I tripped. My knees hit the edge of the top step, and I cried out as my elbows hit the floor. My face burned with embarrassment, and I rolled onto my side and closed my eyes to compose myself. Within seconds Marty was on his knees next to me.

"Beckett, are you okay?" He patted my cheek a few times. "Beckett, say something!" He patted harder.

Footsteps pounded up the stairs, and I opened my eyes to both Marty and Todd eyeing me with concern.

"I think I'm fine. Just shaken up." I pushed into a partial sitting position and gave them a wavering smile.

Marty sighed with relief. "Let's get you up, then."

The two men helped me to my feet. Then Todd headed back downstairs, and Marty pulled me into his arms. I sank into his embrace and wrapped my arms around him, as I was trembling from the experience and my knees and elbows were throbbing. He pulled me in tighter and swept one hand up and down my back a few times before loosening his grip and sliding his hands up to my jawline.

His gaze flickered from my eyes to my lips a few times, and I held my breath as the air fairly crackled between us. His desire-filled eyes asked for permission as he tilted his head slowly down toward my own. I didn't help close the distance, but to my surprise, I also couldn't force myself to pull away as all my nerve endings tingled.

The bell over the front door dinged again, bringing me back to reality, and I jerked backward out of Marty's arms. We both glanced down the stairs to find Edna Thorn, the newspaper editor, staring up at us. She raised her eyebrows, and my frantic gaze shot back to Marty.

"Let's go to your office," I said.

He reached toward me as if to take my hand in his.

I shook my head. "We need to talk."

Marty briefly closed his eyes and then followed me to the back of the building and into his office. He shut the door behind us, but neither of us sat. Instead, we stared at each other across his black metal desk.

He shoved his hands into the pockets of his jeans. "I take it you didn't want that to happen?" He nodded toward the door.

I didn't know if I wanted it to happen or not, but I knew it shouldn't. I twisted my hands together. "I'm aware my actions just now might have given you the wrong impression."

He pursed his lips. "As well as yesterday outside the bank?"

I nodded. My seemingly innocent action of reaching for his hand the day before had undoubtedly started this chain of events, and I had done nothing to stop them. I was in a mess of my own making.

"I like you, Marty. You're a good friend. You're a good man." He truly was. There wasn't a more upstanding, conscientious man in Cherry Hill, with the possible exception of Darren. And I couldn't deny the attraction I felt a minute earlier. I realized if it weren't for Mitchell, I would almost certainly be kissing Marty in his office at that very moment instead of having an awkward conversation. My face heated at the revelation.

Marty slid his hands out of his pockets and crossed his arms in front of his chest. "But ..."

I wished I could tell him I didn't like him as anything more than a friend, but I was no longer sure that was true, so I stuck with the facts. "But I'm dating someone."

His arms fell to his sides, and he dropped into his chair. "Who?" His brow furrowed. "Jeff? Kyle?"

I laughed. "I thought you knew me better than that."

"Apparently I don't know you as well as I thought I did," he retorted.

My smile disappeared. "Sorry." I took a deep breath. "It's Mitchell Crowe."

"The detective."

"Yes." I sat on the folding chair across the desk from him.

He tipped his chair onto its back legs as his cool gaze swept over me. "How long has this been going on?"

"It's complicated."

"Try me."

"You really want to know?" I massaged my still-throbbing knees.

Marty's gaze dropped to my hands and shot back up to my face. "I do. I wish I had known this a few minutes ago, that's for sure. I feel like an absolute fool. I would never have touched you if I'd known." He gritted his teeth. *"Never."*

I ordered myself not to cry. "I know, and I'm sorry I put you in that situation." I took a deep breath. "This is all my fault. I should have realized I needed to tell you about Mitchell, but I thought you and I were just friends."

He closed his eyes for a moment. "I'm as much to blame. I should have made my feelings clear before now."

I nodded. "I've been told I'm oblivious when it comes to men."

One corner of his mouth curved up, but he didn't fully smile.

I continued, "The thing with Mitchell started back in March, though. Not recently."

The front legs of his chair hit the ground, and his eyes flashed. "I am really out of the loop."

"You're not. Nobody knew except Aunt Star, Trixie, and Darren. Well, a lot of people knew he was my date for my class reunion, but you know how that turned out."

He nodded and didn't say a word while I explained the entire situation to him.

"That's why I couldn't talk about it," I said. "And even though it started in March, we're only now able to date like normal people." I was surprised he hadn't heard about Mitchell and me at The Blue Barn the previous evening. No doubt someone would tell him before the week was out, but he wouldn't hear it from me.

"I hope it works out for you," he said stiffly.

I narrowed my eyes at him. "I don't think you mean that, and I understand why. But I appreciate you saying it." I tilted my head. "Can we still be friends?"

His eyes searched mine and his gaze moved to my mouth before shifting away from me. "I don't know."

My chest tightened at his response. I didn't want to lose our friendship, but I understood his reluctance. I wasn't positive we could make it work, either. "Fair enough. And I truly am sorry I didn't tell you about Mitchell before now." I stood and opened the door, but he remained seated and still wouldn't look me in the eye.

"See you soon?" I asked hopefully.

"Can't avoid each other in this town. Goodbye, Beckett."

Hearing him say my name was like a punch to the gut. Marty was one of the few people in Cherry Hill who made an effort to call me Beckett instead of my childhood nickname of Becky.

I gave him a wobbly smile. "Bye."

"Close the door, will you?"

I pulled the door shut behind me and took a few shaky breaths before heading back downstairs. I plastered on a smile in case I ran into anyone I knew.

Chapter Twelve

"Detective Crowe called again," Greg informed me when I entered the church office. "Said he was on a lunch recess, whatever that means. Something tells me he's not in elementary school."

I was too upset about what had happened with Marty to be disappointed I missed Mitchell's call or to be irritated by Greg's statement.

"He's in court today," I explained. "Did he say he'd call back?" If so, I hoped it wouldn't be soon, because he would quickly detect something was wrong, and there was no way I could tell him about Marty. This situation was much different than the one with Jeff.

"He said to tell you he would call tonight. I told him you'd be here with me to help with youth group for a couple hours."

I nodded and dropped my purse on my desk. Then I sank down into my chair and stared at the filing cabinets.

Greg moved into my line of vision. "You okay?"

My eyes filled with tears. "No."

His hands fisted, as if he wanted to reach out to me but knew he couldn't. How had I managed to be surrounded by men who had feelings for me? I needed a hug, but not from Greg.

Pastor Coker's office door opened, and his eyes widened when he spotted me. He rushed around my desk and pulled me up out of my chair and into his arms. Tears rushed out of me in a flood and onto his shirt.

He patted me on the back. "What's wrong, my dear?"

"I c-c-can't tell you."

"Okay ... can you tell Mrs. Coker?"

She wasn't my first choice, but she would do, since my other options were at work. "Uh-huh." I sniffled.

"Greg, call the parsonage and see if my wife's there."

Pastor Coker held me with one arm and pulled a clean handkerchief out of his pocket with the other as Greg made the call.

He greeted Veronica but didn't know what else to say. "Hold on." He put his hand over the mouthpiece. "What do I tell her?"

"Tell her Beckett will be there in two minutes."

Greg relayed the message and hung up.

Pastor Coker sat me back down in my chair, and I dried my face with the hanky.

"Th-thank you."

"I'll walk you over there when you're ready."

After I composed myself, I shakily stood. He took me by the arm and led me out.

We entered the back door of the Cokers' home, and Veronica bustled into the kitchen. When she saw my face, she pulled me away from her husband and into her arms. "I've got it from here."

Pastor Coker patted my shoulder and left us.

Veronica held me as I cried some more and then moved me to a chair at the kitchen table. She handed me a box of tissues, poured us each a glass of iced tea, and sat across from me.

"Tell me what's wrong."

I took a sip of my tea and opened my mouth to speak, but tears began falling again. "I d-d-don't know what's wrong with me."

"There's nothing wrong with you, honey. A lot has happened the last two days. All those varying emotions can be overwhelming. Tell me what tipped you over the edge."

I dried my eyes and told her the condensed version of what happened with Marty. When I finished, I said, "He's been a great friend the past few months. I don't want to lose him." My eyes filled with tears again, and I looked at the ceiling to try to contain them. "I truly didn't realize I was leading him on."

"I know you didn't. And I'm sure once he has time to start thinking clearly, he will, too. He'll come around. He's a good man."

I picked at a hangnail instead of looking at her. "He's an excellent man."

Veronica hesitated before asking, "Do you have feelings for Marty? Is that why you're so upset about this?"

I still couldn't look at her. "Maybe."

She sighed. "Goodness. Did you want him to kiss you?"

"I wish I could say no, but I knew he was going to kiss me, and I couldn't make myself pull away until Edna came in."

"Oh, dear. Do you feel more strongly for him than for Mitchell?"

I briefly closed my eyes. "No." I bit my lip. "I don't know. I didn't realize I might have feelings for Marty until this happened. But it's different than the way I feel about Mitchell. With Mitchell it's all fireworks. I get all ... you know ... tingly when I'm with him."

Veronica smiled. "Tingly?"

I smiled back and wiggled my shoulders. "Tingly. He makes me feel things I haven't felt in a long time. But I don't know him very well yet. We've talked a lot, and I know a lot of facts about him, but I haven't been able to spend much time with him or see how he interacts with people—or even that much with me—when he's not in detective mode."

"And when you're with Marty?" She took a drink of tea.

"It's comfortable. I can be myself with him. He's an excellent listener." My throat began to close up, but I swallowed and pressed on. "He's kind and considerate and understanding. I mean, the man forgave me for suspecting him of Aidan's murder—not after months or years, but almost immediately. Even when I told him about Mitchell, he didn't lash out at me. Was he angry? Yes, I could see it in his eyes. But he stayed calm. He didn't take out his anger on me. Who wouldn't want to be with a man like that?" I couldn't believe what I was revealing to her—and to myself—but every bit of it was true.

Veronica surveyed me with sharp eyes as she tapped her fingernails on her glass. "And were there tingles with him?"

I looked down at my lap and nodded. "There were just now. I guess I didn't feel it before because I hadn't considered him in that way. We didn't become friends until after I met Mitchell, so it never even crossed my mind that we could be more. But then Aunt Star's comments yesterday got me thinking about it, and here we are."

I took a deep breath. "Marty's an attractive man. I hate to admit it felt good when he held me—not exactly the same as with Mitchell, but still good. It felt natural. I most definitely wasn't repulsed by his actions." I put my hand on my chest. "And my heart hurts when I think he might not be part of my life anymore."

"You are in a bit of a predicament," Veronica said, "but let's consider this logically. You need both passion and friendship for a strong relationship with a man. Do you have a friendship with Mitchell, or is it all fireworks?"

"Both," I said. "But that's true for both men. With

Mitchell, it's more fireworks, but we're working on the friendship part. And with Marty, it's more friendship."

Veronica cocked her head to the side. "I can't make this decision for you, but I don't know that you should toss away what you have with Mitchell because of a friend you may or may not have feelings for."

She held up a hand to keep me from responding to her statement. "I know right now you think you do, but it's been an emotional couple of days. I don't know that you can fully trust your feelings right now. I think you should see where things are going to lead with Mitchell. Find out if it's going to be one of your I-need-to-fix-him relationships or not. Marty isn't going anywhere. Trust me."

"But do I tell Mitchell about Marty?"

"I don't know that I would tell him everything you told me. No good would come of it, and it's all so new you don't even fully know how you feel right now. As for whether to tell him the basic facts of what happened with Marty, that's up to you."

I stuck my pinky nail between my teeth while I pondered the situation.

"I'm not going to lie to him, but I also don't think it would be fair to Marty to tell Mitchell anything that happened unless he asks. Marty's actions were innocent. But there's no way for Mitchell to know what happened, so I don't know why he would ask." I didn't plan to tell anyone else about Marty—not even Aunt Star, if I could help it. And I was certain Marty wouldn't mention it to anyone.

"There's your answer."

"I feel like I've betrayed Mitchell, though. I should have pulled away as soon as Marty put his arms around me."

"You no more betrayed that man than you betrayed Bugs Bunny. Don't let yourself think so for one minute. You were letting a friend comfort you. You had no idea how Marty felt at the time."

I gave Veronica a weak smile. "I kind of did, but I was in denial. Thanks for helping me talk through this. I feel better about it now. Not great, but better. Can we keep this all between us, though? Nobody else needs to know."

"My lips are sealed. I won't even bring it up with you again, but if you need to talk about it, I am always here. You can call me anytime—day or night."

"Thanks." I groaned. "What do I do about Edna, though?"

"You're sure she saw you?"

"Positive." I hung my head. "And she also saw us when Marty's arm was around me outside the bank yesterday."

Veronica gave me an exasperated look. "Why was his arm around you?"

I told her about our interactions after the robbery.

"And none of that tipped you off about his interest in you?" She shook her head.

"No, but Aunt Star caught on. I simply refused to believe it when she told me."

"You think Edna will spread the news?"

"I don't think so, but I probably should talk to her."

"I'm not sure that's the best idea, if you prefer she forget about it. But if you do, what will you say?"

I slumped in my seat. "No idea."

"Why don't you put that conversation on the back burner for now? I think it's time to get your mind off men and back onto the investigation. Did you learn anything from Jeff at lunch?"

I gave her the highlights of our lunch conversation.

"That does rather put the spotlight on Aggie," Veronica said. "But that Banner girl is a contender. I went to chat with Darren about what I saw, and he asked me several questions I hadn't considered."

"Like what? Oh! First, does Kimberly still have long hair?"

"Why?"

I explained Jeff's theory about the woman robber's hair.

"That makes sense," Veronica said, "but a lot of people have long hair."

"I said the same thing."

"But it couldn't be too long, or she couldn't have hidden it under the ski mask."

"Great point. So was Kimberly's hair long?"

"Her hair was pulled back, so it was long, but I don't know how long."

I nodded. "What did Darren ask?"

"He wanted to know which way they were heading, what they were wearing, and if I could see their expressions."

"And?"

"They were heading toward downtown. I think his shirt was black. Hers was definitely a light blue T-shirt. They looked upset."

"Interesting—the upset part, I mean. Maybe he was forcing her to do it, and she didn't want to."

"Or perhaps," Veronica said, "they were two innocent young people having an argument about anything else under the sun."

"Possibly. But let's pretend they're the robbers. She's not the type to wear a baggy black sweatshirt out in public, so she probably wouldn't put it on until the last minute. I still have no idea what her motive could be."

"Do you know who her friends are here in town?" she asked. "Anybody you could talk to and find out if she needs money or has an issue with the bank or Perry?"

"Kimberly was on the volleyball team, so Trixie might be able to help." My best friend was the varsity girls' volleyball coach at Cherry Hill High. "I'll call her tonight after she's home from practice."

"Did you figure out who this Sam person is that Jacqui's dating?" Veronica asked.

"No, and I have no way to find out. I can't very well call up Suzanne and ask for his last name without her figuring out I suspect her daughter of robbing the bank—and her."

"True."

"I don't know anybody in Taylorville well enough to call up and ask them, either. Do you? Are you friends with any pastors' wives over there?"

She patted the table. "Yes, I am. I'll call my friend Jean and see if she can help us out."

"Awesome." I pushed up from my seat. "I need to get back over to church. I've barely done any work the last two days."

"You might want to freshen up before you leave." She circled her fingers around her eyes.

I could only imagine the current state of my eye makeup. I hurried down the hall to the bathroom and washed my face. I also removed my tights and tossed them in the trash can, as both knees had holes in them, resulting in runners all the way up and down.

"Thanks again for your help," I said to Veronica when I was ready to head out.

Veronica followed me to the door. "Anytime. Really."

I threw my arms around her and gave her a tight squeeze. "I'm glad we're friends."

She laughed. "Me, too, my girl. Me, too."

Pastor Coker and Greg tiptoed around me when I returned, and thankfully neither of them asked me how I was feeling. I wouldn't have known what to say if they had. I didn't have much work to do, which was frustrating. There was no Bible lesson to study for youth group, as we planned to spend the evening decorating the fellowship hall for the Halloween party.

I desperately needed a distraction. I usually didn't type up the Sunday bulletin until Thursday afternoon, in case somebody needed to make a change, but I went ahead and did it to give myself something to do. Then I made the copies on the ditto machine, and Greg helped me fold them.

"Have you heard anything about Mr. Adamson today?" Greg asked after a minute of silence.

"As of early this morning he was the same as yesterday—not better, but not worse."

"Your mom doing okay with everything?"

"Yes. She's worried about Perry, but she's the most resilient woman I know."

It suddenly occurred to me that since Greg often subbed at the high school, he might know Kimberly.

"Last spring, did you ever sub in a class with Kimberly Banner in it?"

"Coach Banner's daughter? Yes. She was a good kid. And she was kind. Didn't ever make fun of the sub's hair." He grinned and ran his hand down the back of his head, where the hair was longer than in the front. Though he was self-conscious of his haircut earlier in the year, he had grown more confident in his hairstyle choice.

I laughed. "That's the sign of a truly kind person."

"Why are you asking about Kimberly?"

I hesitated. "You'll keep this to yourself, right?"

"Of course."

I told him our suspicions about her.

"Wow. I don't know what to say," Greg said. "Surely it's a coincidence she was in town yesterday morning."

"That's what I'm hoping, but I don't know. Did she have a boyfriend last spring?"

"I don't know about an official boyfriend, but she went to

prom with Cory Hankins." Greg was a prom chaperone. He had asked me to join him, but I declined, concerned he would see it as a date.

"But she's older than him," I said.

"It's not illegal for women to date younger men," he replied testily. He focused on a bulletin instead of me, but I knew what he was getting at, as he was a few years younger than me.

"Yes, I know, but it's not very common—especially in high school. Cory, huh? This is a very interesting turn of events."

"Why?"

"Because Cory's dad is a suspect."

"Steve Hankins?" Greg shook his head. "No way. He would never rob a bank. If he found a wallet on the street, he'd find the owner and return it. He might even add money to it."

"How do you know Steve so well?" Cory went to youth group back when Greg was first hired, but he hadn't been around recently. And Steve didn't attend church—at least not ours.

"I started playing basketball with the guys on Saturdays. Sometimes we grab breakfast at The Check afterward."

"How did I not know that?" A group of local men, including Darren and Trixie's husband Scott, played basketball at the high school gym every Saturday morning.

"There's a lot of things you don't know about me," he said petulantly.

I'd about had it with men for the day, but I bit back a retort and folded papers silently as tension built in the room. I finally decided to go for it. If I didn't lay everything on the line now, I might never muster up the courage to do so again.

"Greg?"

"Yes?"

I stopped folding and looked him in the eye. "I would like us to be friends—just friends—without you consistently referencing the fact you want us to be more. We won't be more. Even if Mitchell and I were to break up, you and I won't ever be more." I hated being so blunt, but I needed to be, and I was in no mood to go gentle on him. I was gentle before, and that didn't work anyway. "You need to overcome your feelings for me, or you need to hide them around me. But stop dropping hints, start respecting my choice to not date you, and quit feeling sorry for yourself. There are plenty of other women in this world. You need to find one."

Chapter Thirteen

G reg gaped at me like I'd slapped him. He probably would have preferred if I had. His mouth opened and closed a few times, but no words came out. I was tempted to apologize for my tirade, but I stopped myself. The awkwardness between us had to end.

Finally he said in a strained voice, "I'm sorry. It's ... I've never felt this strongly about someone before. I don't know what to do."

Despite myself, my heart went out to him. Thankfully I kept from reaching out to touch him.

"I know what you need to do," I said.

"You do?"

"Yes. Talk to Mrs. Coker about it."

He barked out a laugh. "Are you kidding me?"

"Not at all. She's great at giving advice about stuff like this. Trust me, I know. Go talk to her. She'll help you deal with your feelings, and she might even find you a woman who adores you. You deserve that, Greg."

He gave me an incredulous look and started to respond,

but I held up a hand to stop him, picked up the phone, and dialed the parsonage.

"Mrs. Coker? I'm sending Greg over to you. He'll be there in a minute." I hung up before she could ask any questions.

"Go. Tell her everything. She won't breathe a word of it to anyone else—including me. I promise. The woman is a vault with stuff like this."

He nodded and left the office. He was probably afraid of what would happen if he didn't.

Pastor Coker's office door slowly opened, and he popped his head out. "He's gone?"

"Yes. Did you hear everything?"

"I couldn't tune it out. You get loud when you're feisty."

My face turned red. "I'm sorry."

He settled into the chair across from my desk. "Don't be sorry. He needed to hear it. In fact, I should have had that conversation with him, but I was too much of a coward to get involved. I'm the one who should be sorry. I guess I thought he'd finally grow out of his infatuation."

"I thought he would, too."

"Veronica will set him straight."

I grinned. "She certainly will."

"I got myself a good one, didn't I?"

"You sure did." A year earlier I wouldn't have meant that statement. Veronica could be curt and pushy and closed off. But we'd grown closer throughout the year, and I had discovered her true nature. She truly was a good woman and an excellent friend.

Thirty minutes later, Pastor Coker left to visit Perry at the hospital, with a promise to call with an update after he arrived, and I was once again left with nothing to do but sit and wait for the phone to ring.

It didn't.

I pulled my suspect notebook out of my purse and updated my notes. Then I grabbed Greg's latest youth ministry book off the shelf and attempted to read, but my thoughts kept wandering—to Mitchell, to the case, to Marty, to Perry, and back again. I was wondering how things were going with Greg and Veronica when the office door opened.

Veronica entered and plopped down into Greg's desk chair. "My relationship advice business is closed for the day."

I giggled. Her exasperated look made me laugh again, which turned into belly laughs, and Veronica soon joined in. By the time I got myself under control, tears streamed down my cheeks.

"Oh, I needed that laugh," I said.

She wiped her eyes. "Me, too."

We smiled at each other across the office.

I cocked my head. "Did you set him straight?"

"That's between him and me."

"Good. I told him you're a vault. Glad to know I didn't lie."

"You really let him have it."

"I had reached my limit with men for the day."

She burst out laughing again. "I hope you're not home if Mitchell calls you tonight."

I grinned. "If I am, he won't know what hit him." I sobered when I recalled telling him he was the only man I wanted to date.

"What? Why do you have that look on your face?"

"I can't tell you. You're closed, remember?"

"I can make an after-hours exception if you need me to." She smirked at me. "But it'll cost you some cookies tomorrow."

I decided I didn't lie to Mitchell when I said I didn't want to date anyone else, because I believed it to be true at the time. "No, I'm good."

"You sure? Or are you just trying to get out of baking cookies tonight?"

"Maybe a little bit of both. Where is Greg, by the way?"

"I sent him home. I figured he wouldn't want to be here in the office with you this afternoon."

"Yeah, that would have been more than a little awkward. Youth group tonight is going to be a barrel of laughs." I wished I could get out of going, but I was the one with the decorating plan for the Halloween party. "In other news, guess what I learned from Greg before I ripped his head off."

"I have zero energy for guessing games." She set her elbows on Greg's desk and propped her chin on her hands.

"Kimberly Banner and Cory Hankins went to prom together."

"No!"

"Yep. Do you think Cory could be the driver of the car?"

She thought for a moment. "Maybe. But wouldn't he have been in school?"

"Kimberly should have been in school, too. I'll ask Trixie if she knows whether Cory was absent yesterday. I don't know if he's in one of her classes this year, but he could be. She might also know what kind of car he drives."

Veronica said, "So Cory could have motive, if his parents are having financial problems."

"And we know he was getting into trouble a lot last spring due to all the drama with Aidan both before and after he died."

"And Kimberly has insider knowledge about the bank."

"They have motive and opportunity—if Cory skipped school—and almost anyone could have means. Pretty much every family around here has a gun or five. And ski masks, gloves, and duffel bags are easy to come by. Oh! Did I tell you

Marvin said the woman was wearing gloves, and the man wasn't wearing a wedding ring? That keeps Cory in the picture."

"Do you honestly think Kimberly and Cory could be the 80s version of Bonnie and Clyde?" she asked.

"Stranger things have happened in Cherry Hill, as we well know. Did you talk to your friend in Taylorville about Jacqui's boyfriend?"

She hit her forehead with her palm. "How could I forget to tell you? His name is Sam Dalrymple."

"Dalrymple?"

"Sure enough. Jean said he's a good-looking fellow, but he's been in and out of trouble with the law his entire adult life, including some breaking and entering. He's around Jacqui's age—a few years older than you. And he's currently unemployed."

"How does your friend know so much about him?"

"He grew up in their church. His mom is good friends with Jean. She said his sister is a mess, too. Strung out on drugs half the time."

"Did you tell her we suspect him of the robbery?"

"No, I told her I'm friends with Suzanne and she had concerns about what kind of man her daughter was dating. Which is true—just not the whole truth."

I opened my suspect notebook and turned to a fresh page. "Let's go through our suspects again. We've got Jacqui and Sam." I scribbled their names. "Kimberly and Cory. I think we can cross Steve off the list. Greg was right. The man doesn't have it in him."

"I agree. Even with all the shocking events we've experienced lately, I can't see Steve doing it, either."

"Then we've got Aggie, who also had means, motive, and opportunity. Her partner could be this boyfriend everyone at the bank has heard about but never seen. I wish we knew more about her, and why she left Springfield. I wonder what bank she worked at down there."

"How could we find out?" Veronica asked.

"I bet Jeff knows! Or at least he can maybe look at her job application to find out. Let me call him."

I rang the bank, and my mother answered. "Hey, Mom, can I talk to Jeff for a minute?"

"Why?"

"Because."

"Why?"

"Really? We're doing this?"

"I'm waiting." I could imagine Mom putting a hand on her hip.

"Ugh. Fine. Can anyone else hear me?"

"No."

"We're wondering where Aggie worked in Springfield. It's probably on her job application, if Jeff still has it."

"Ah, good idea. I'll transfer you over to him. See how easy that was?"

I rolled my eyes and waited for Jeff to answer.

"This is Jeff."

"Hi, it's Beckett. Do you know where Aggie worked in Springfield? Which bank?"

"Hang on a sec ... okay, had to shut my door. Let me pull her job application out of my files."

I tapped my fingernails on my desk as I waited.

"Will you please stop the tapping?" Veronica requested.

"Sorry." I stilled my fingers.

"Huh?" Jeff said.

"Wasn't talking to you. Carry on."

"Who's with you?"

"Ver—uh, Mrs. Coker."

"She's in on this investigation, too?"

"She always is. She's my trusty sidekick."

I smirked at Veronica, and she snorted in disdain, but I could tell she was holding back a smile.

"Here we go," Jeff said. "Battlefield Savings Bank. Got a pen to write down the number?"

"Sure do."

He rattled off the phone number and I copied it into my notebook.

"Thanks."

"I guess I should tell Darren this, too," Jeff said.

"Yeah. Maybe make a copy of the entire application on that new photocopier you have over there, and take it to him." I wished the church had a photocopier instead of the ancient ditto machine. I wondered if they would cut a deal for me to make the bulletin copies at the bank.

"Will do."

"All right, I need to make this call. Talk to you soon." I hung up.

"What are you going to say when you call?" Veronica inquired.

"Hmm. Maybe I'll ask to talk to her, and I'll see how they respond. Then I'll go from there."

"Well, go on. We haven't got all day."

"Yes, ma'am." I dialed the number.

"Hullo," a gruff male voice said.

"Um, hello, is this Battlefield Savings Bank?"

Silence.

"Hello?"

"You have the wrong number."

Click.

I stared at the handset and hung it up.

Veronica raised her eyebrows. "Well?"

"Wrong number."

"How was it the wrong number?"

"How am I supposed to know?"

"Call Jeff back and make sure you wrote it down right."

I knew I did, but I called anyway. Thankfully Jeff answered instead of my mom.

"It's me," I said. "I think I wrote the number down wrong. Can you give it to me again?"

He said the same number as before.

"That's the number I called. A man answered, and I asked if it was the bank, and he was quiet for a few seconds before telling me it was the wrong number."

Veronica jumped in. "Ask him if he called the number before they gave her the job."

I repeated the question to Jeff.

"I don't know. Perry would have been the one to call."

"Well, that doesn't help us."

"We need to get to the bottom of this little problem," Jeff said, "whether she's the robber or not. If she lied on her job application, that's grounds for termination. I'll find the real number for the bank and call to see if she's ever worked there. I'll let you know."

As I was hanging up, Jeff's voice faintly said, "Wait!"

I put the phone back to my ear. "Yes?"

"When you hang up, call back over here and talk to your mom. Tell her to keep Aggie occupied on their side of the lobby, so she can't possibly overhear my conversation."

"Got it."

I called right back and gave the instructions to Mom, who shockingly agreed without a detailed explanation.

Brrrring!

I snatched up the phone, expecting it to be Jeff. "Yes?"

"Beckett?"

"Sorry, Pastor. I didn't use my usual greeting because I thought I knew who was calling. What can I help you with?"

"I'm calling to give you an update on Perry."

"Oh! Yes, how's he doing?"

"He took a turn for the worse about twenty minutes ago. They said they don't expect him to make it through the night."

Tears filled my eyes for the twenty-seventh time that day. "Oh, no."

"Sandra wants Jeff to know, so he can come, but she doesn't want him to hear it over the phone. Would you be comfortable going to tell him? I guess everybody else over at the bank needs to know, too."

"Of course I can. Thanks for letting us know."

"Bad news?" Veronica asked when I hung up.

I filled her in and then stood but didn't move toward the door. "I don't want to tell him. Can you do it?"

"Nobody wants that job. But the two of you are friends, right? He should hear it from you instead of from a near stranger."

I sighed. "You're right."

She opened the door and motioned me over. Then she hugged me and pushed me out into the hall. "You can do it."

As I slowly made my way down the sidewalk toward the bank, I glanced across the street and spotted Marty through the hardware store window. He caught my eye but didn't smile or wave. He simply watched me with a neutral expression. I turned my gaze back in front of me and willed myself not to cry.

Chapter Fourteen

I took a deep breath before pushing through the bank doors. Jeff's office door and blinds were closed, so I assumed he was still on the phone with the bank in Springfield. Aggie was assisting a customer, and Mom was chatting with Christine.

If Jeff was still on the phone, I didn't want to disturb him. Since Aggie was occupied for the moment, I figured it would be okay for me to talk to Mom privately. I approached her and Christine.

"Mom, can we talk in the break room for a minute?"

"Sure."

She stepped away from Christine and followed me down the hallway. I sat at the small round table in the break room, and Mom took the chair across from me.

She looked at me worriedly. "What's this about, honey?"

"It's Perry."

Mom put a hand on her chest. "Don't tell me ..."

I managed to choke out, "He's not going to make it through the night," before tears began streaming down my face.

Mom moved to the chair next to me, wrapped her arms around me, and cried like I'd never seen her cry before—not even when my grandparents had passed away. She typically dealt with her pain and grief in stony silence.

"Ladies, what's going on?"

I couldn't recall ever hearing Jeff sound scared before. He stood in the doorway with a look of dread. Mom leapt up, pulled him into the room, and shut the door. Then she wrapped her arms around him.

I steeled myself for what I was about to say. "Perry took a turn for the worse. You need to go to the hospital." I stumbled to my feet and put my arms around both of them as we all sobbed.

"Mom," I pleaded through my tears, "will you take him? Don't let him go alone."

"Of course. Your dad will want to go, too."

Jeff broke away from us and tore a paper towel off the roll by the sink to wipe his face. "I can't leave until the bank is closed."

"We'll close early," Mom declared as she dried her own tears.

"We can't. It's against policy."

"Policy, my hiney." Mom looked at her watch. "How about this? When the lobby closes in twenty minutes, we'll be done for the day. We'll put a sign on the drive-through window telling customers to drop their deposits through the slot. People will understand. It's too late to process any deposits today anyway."

Jeff hesitated. "But what if people need to withdraw money?"

"We can open early tomorrow, if you think that will help. We can put it on the sign."

"All right." He closed his eyes. "I guess I need to tell the rest of the employees about this, don't I?"

"You do not," Mom said. "I'm doing it." She marched out the door. As she pulled it shut behind her, she said to Jeff, "Take all the time you need."

He collapsed into a chair, and I took the seat across from him. I reached a hand across the table, and he clasped it between his own.

"I'm so sorry, Jeff."

He nodded. "Thank you for coming to tell me in person. I can't imagine hearing the news over the phone. How'd you find out?"

"Pastor Coker is there. Sandra asked him to see if I could come tell you." I looked down. "I didn't want to, but I also didn't *not* want to."

His eyes glistened, and he pressed his hands against mine before letting go and wiping his tears away.

"I know this might not be the best time," I said quietly, "but what did you find out about Aggie?"

"They've never heard of her. I'm going to have to let her go, but I'm not going to deal with her until tomorrow. And I need to tell the police." He paused. "Ah, shoot. I'm supposed to go talk to Darren after work."

"I'll go. Put the paperwork in an envelope for me to give him."

"Thanks. Tell him I'll talk to him tomorrow if he has any questions or if he needs to hear any of it directly from me. By the way, what happened to your knees? And weren't you wearing red pantyhose earlier?"

My bare knees were still pink, and one had a scrape on it from the metal edging of the stairs.

"I fell going up some steps. You know me."

"You fell going *up* the steps?"

"What can I say? I'm talented." I struck a silly pose and got the laugh I hoped for.

Jeff's smile dimmed quickly. "I need to call the board and tell them about Perry."

"Who's the board president? I'll call them, and they can let everyone else know. You don't need to worry about anything but Perry right now."

"It's Stan Jones." He cocked his head. "Why are you being so nice to me?"

"Because I just can't help it." I grinned at him. "And because you're my friend. This is what friends do."

"I need to get some more friends like you."

"I'll make sure and tell Randy and Kyle you said that."

Darren's eyes registered surprise when Barbara sent me back to his office. When I told him why I was there, he escorted me to an interview room so he could record the conversation, and he asked Frank to join us.

I told them everything Mom and Jeff disclosed about Aggie. Darren asked a few questions throughout, but he didn't seem overly excited about anything I had to say. Then I handed him the envelope from Jeff and explained about the phone calls to Springfield.

"Beckett Monahan, why didn't you lead with this?"

"I don't know. I guess because it's the last thing that happened. I was giving you the information in order!"

"Next time, please start with the most incriminating information." He handed the papers to Frank. "Get on the phone with the Springfield Police Department. Find out everything you can about this woman."

"Will do, boss." Frank scuttled off.

"Why didn't you already do that?" I asked.

"We had no concrete reason to suspect her. We would have

gotten to it, but we had other leads that seemed more promising."

"Like Kimberly Banner?"

He shrugged.

"Have you talked to Aunt Star today?"

"Yes. She stopped by and told me I needed to talk to Jeff, but I was in the middle of something, so we didn't chat. Why?"

"No reason. Anyway, did you know Kimberly went to prom with Cory Hankins?"

His eyebrows twitched briefly before settling back into their normal state. He hadn't known. "Why do you think that's relevant?"

"Because his parents are having financial problems. And he kind of went off the rails when everything happened with Aidan. You might want to find out if he was at school yesterday."

"Oh, I might, huh?"

"Just a suggestion."

"I'll take it into consideration. Anything else I might want to do?"

"Yes, Jacqui's boyfriend is Sam Dalrymple. From what I've heard, he has a record and is currently unemployed."

Darren wrote Sam's name down. "That it?"

"For the moment."

"So were you talking about Aggie when you were holed up with Jeff in his office this morning?"

I was tempted to say yes, which was technically true because I had mentioned Aggie to Jeff that morning. But since I was in a police interrogation room, I figured I shouldn't stretch the truth. "No. How did you know about that?"

"Can't say."

The only people who even knew I talked to Jeff were Mom,

Aggie, and Christine. Darren obviously had not talked to Aggie. I wondered when and why he talked to Christine. I opened my mouth to ask, but he held up a hand.

"Like I said, I can't say. What did you and Jeff talk about?"

"That's none of your business."

"Beckett, this is a major investigation. It may even become a murder investigation. Everything that happens at the bank is my business."

"We talked about Perry, okay? And about Jeff cleaning his blood off the floor."

He closed his eyes. "Ah. Yes. Again, I'm sorry." He opened his eyes and raised an eyebrow. "But why did you need to close the door and blinds?"

I narrowed my eyes at him. "I can't say."

He glared at me.

"Doesn't feel good, does it?" I taunted.

"No offense, but you don't look good on a high horse, my friend."

"Sorry." I sighed. "Jeff needed privacy, is all."

Understanding dawned in his eyes. "Got it."

"But that's all between me and you."

Darren pointed to his right, and my eyes followed.

I groaned. "And the tape recorder. Can you rewind it?"

"No can do."

I mouthed to him, "Can you stop it?"

"Interview ended." Darren stated the time and stopped the machine.

"Please don't let Mitchell know about me and Jeff talking in his office. We didn't do anything inappropriate, but Mitchell is a little wary of Jeff."

"I won't tell him if I don't need to. But I can't promise he won't read about it in a transcript or listen to one of the tapes. If he does, you need to hope he'll understand."

I nodded and looked down at my lap. Darren's hand slid across the table and stopped right in front of me. My focus moved to it and then up to his face.

"Have the two of you talked about whether you're free to date other people?"

My eyes widened at the personal nature of his question, but I answered. "Yes, and we're only dating each other."

"Then if Mitchell doesn't trust you and doesn't understand you were only helping a friend, that's not good. You know that, right?"

"I do." I took a deep breath. "Do you have reason to think he won't?"

"He's an excellent detective, but I don't know what he's like outside of work. We don't talk about anything other than our cases. Well, except talking about you from time to time ... which pains me to no end." He gave me a crooked smile. "I'm not saying don't trust him. He seems like an okay guy. But I am saying be careful and don't be overly trusting."

"You're sure there's not something you're not telling me about him?"

"I'm sure. But if I ever discover anything about him that would make me think he might consider doing, saying, or even thinking something that has the potential to hurt you, you'll be the first to know. After I punch him in the nose, of course."

"Of course." I smiled and headed toward the door. "You're a good man, Darren Turley. And you just proved you'll be an amazing uncle to me someday."

His jaw dropped, and I flounced out of the room before he could formulate a response.

As soon as I thought Trixie might be home from volleyball practice, I called her house from my bedroom phone.

"Wallace residence, Krystal speaking," a childish voice answered.

"Hey there, Krystal. It's Beckett." I flopped back on my flowered bedspread.

"Hi! Wanna know what happened at school today?" Trixie's nine-year-old daughter asked. "It's soooo exciting!"

"I've never wanted to hear anything more."

Krystal giggled. "My class is going to do a play, and I got the biggest part!"

"That's awesome! I'm proud of you, kiddo."

"I have lines to memorize, so I need to get started. You want to talk to Mommy?"

"Sure do. Congratulations on the play."

"Thanks. *Mommy, it's Beckett!*"

I jerked the phone away and rubbed my ear. The next bit of phone etiquette Trixie needed to teach her child was to move the handset away from her mouth before yelling.

"Hey, Beck. Any news about Perry?"

I gave Trixie the latest update.

"Dang. That's rough. What are they going to do at the bank?"

"I'm guessing they'll make Jeff president, but then they'll need another loan officer."

"Hmm. Maybe I'll apply."

"School was that bad today?"

"Both school and practice. The kids were a mess, and it's not even a full moon."

"Speaking of kids being a mess, was Cory Hankins at school yesterday?"

She paused. "Is there a particular reason you're asking that?"

"I'll tell you in a minute. Also, what kind of car does he drive?"

"He drives an old black pickup. No, he was not in class yesterday. And today I sent him to the principal's office during second hour trigonometry. That kid is becoming a real handful. I'm extremely concerned about his future. He didn't turn in his homework, and he mouthed off at me when I asked him why."

My heart stopped, and I sat up. "Did he say why he didn't do it?"

"No, he only said it was none of my business—in very colorful language I will not repeat with two sets of little ears listening."

"Yikes."

"Don't even tell me you think Cory Hankins robbed the bank and shot Perry Adamson."

"I don't want to think it, but it's possible." I fell back against my pillows.

"How? Why? With who?"

"We'll start with the who: Kimberly Banner."

"No way in ... h-e-double-hockey-sticks."

I burst out laughing. "I think Krystal is old enough to spell."

"She might not know what letter a hockey stick looks like, though."

"You are a sports-loving family. I'm pretty sure she does."

"Let's get back on topic. What in the what? Kimberly Banner couldn't have anything to do with it. She's at school in Columbia."

I shook my head, though she couldn't see me. "Not yesterday morning, she wasn't."

"I know for a fact she has classes on Tuesday mornings. She called me a few weeks ago about her math class, which I recall her saying meets on Tuesday and Thursday mornings."

"Veronica saw her."

"Where?"

"Riding through town in a light blue two-door car with a male who may or may not have been Cory Hankins."

Trixie was silent.

"What?" I demanded.

"Missy Hankins drives a light blue two-door car."

Chapter Fifteen

"Very interesting that Cory's mom drives the same kind of car seen twice in possible connection with the robbery," I said to Trixie.

"Surely it's a coincidence."

"Maybe, maybe not. Why did Kimberly call you about her math class?"

"She was failing. She asked if I could tutor her over the phone or on the weekends, but I had to say no. With volleyball and the kids, I don't have time. I encouraged her to find someone on campus. The school has resources for students who need help."

"Did she do well in math classes in high school?" I asked as I twirled the phone cord around my finger.

"She struggled. Honestly, she had trouble with several subjects. She always managed to pull at least C's, so she could play volleyball, but it was a chore. I was surprised she got into Mizzou, but Coach went there, so maybe he had some kind of pull."

I pursed my lips. "Sounds like she might not make it in college."

"Maybe not. She worked at the bank this summer, right? Do you know if she did a good job?"

"Mom never said otherwise, but I don't think it takes a whole lot of skills to be a teller." I paused. "No offense to my mom or other bank tellers. It's not like a church secretary has much room to talk."

"Hey, your job is as legitimate as anyone else's, and not everybody is cut out for it. I could never do what you do. Dealing with people like Suzanne all the time? No thank you."

I laughed. "It's not so bad."

"Not for you. You're a natural at dealing with difficult people you can't send to detention. Me? Not so much. The volleyball girls are more than I can handle most days."

"You love it, and you know it."

"Hold on." Trixie held a short, muffled conversation with her kids over a dispute about a *Star Wars* toy. "I'm back. I love the game, and I love the girls. Their boy drama? Big fat nope."

"Speaking of boy drama ..."

"Oooh! Do tell."

Nothing animated my usually quiet, laid-back friend quite like hearing about my love life, not that there'd been much to tell in the past few years.

"It would take a day to tell it all, because I have dealt with little else for the twenty-four hours since I last talked to you. I am so over men right now."

"Men? In the plural?"

"Four of them, to be exact." I held up four fingers.

Trixie whistled. "Beckett Monahan, I never knew you had it in you."

"Nor did I. Nor do I want to experience a day like today ever again."

"Are you over Mitchell in addition to these other three mystery men?"

"No, but I won't be upset if I don't talk to him tonight. He may even be trying to call me right now, but I don't care enough to end this call and keep the line free." I shrugged.

"I'm glad I mean so much to you. Now, don't leave me hanging. At least tell me who the other three guys are. No, wait. Let me guess."

"Really?"

"I need to live vicariously through you. Getting married and having a baby at nineteen put a damper on my social life."

"I think you're doing fine with Scott and the kids."

"Yeah, yeah. They're great. I love them more than life itself. Now, let's see, Mitchell is contestant number one in the Beckett Dating Game. So contestant number two has to be ... Greg."

"Bingo!"

"As for contestant number three," she paused dramatically, "I'm going with Kyle."

"*Bzzzz.* Surprisingly, no. Though I haven't seen him in a few weeks, so there could be potential," I joked. Kyle was an outrageous flirt.

"We'll leave an extra seat open for him, then. My next guess is Marty."

"*Ding, ding, ding!*"

"That one isn't a surprise."

"No?"

"No. And if you weren't dating Mitchell, I'd tell you to go for it."

I asked nonchalantly, "Why have you never mentioned this before?"

"You didn't want to date anyone when you moved back here, and then Mitchell came along, so ..."

"Right."

"You're being weird. Are you interested in Marty?" Trixie was ridiculously perceptive.

I rolled onto my side. "I don't know."

"Beck! Spill."

I hadn't intended to tell her about Marty, but I couldn't hold out on her. After needlessly swearing her to secrecy, I told her everything.

"You know I like your dreamy detective. But Marty? He's perfect for you."

"Don't say things like that! You're going to confuse me even more."

"Ditch Mitchell and drive yourself out to Marty's house *right now*."

"Trix!" I rolled over onto my back again.

"Okay, okay. Maybe we should consider the situation like the mature adults we supposedly are."

"Veronica said I should see where things go with Mitchell. And if it doesn't work out, Marty will still likely be there."

"She's smart. That's exactly what you should do."

I huffed out a breath. "That is the opposite of what you told me to do twenty seconds ago."

"Don't listen to me. I get too excited about these things. Like I said: no social life."

"I'm a little offended by that statement. Do I not constitute a social life?"

"Sorry. No social life but you, Scott, and the kids," she amended.

"That's better."

"We are not done talking about the Marty situation, but there's yet another contestant I need to identify. Hmm. This one is tough. What other single men would you even have been around today?"

I didn't help her out.

"Please tell me he's not married."

"Not anymore."

"Jeff." She said it as a statement, not a question.

"And you're the winner!" I flung my arm out wide.

"Beck. No."

"Rest assured I am in no way interested in dating Jeff Jenkins ever again."

"I'm extremely relieved to hear it."

"I can't tell you what happened with him today, because I promised."

"Of course you did. Just to spite me."

I laughed. "Seriously, Trix, I can't give you details. But I did let him down in no uncertain terms."

"Good. What about Greg? Did you let him down, too?"

I filled her in on what happened with Greg.

"So there's two contestants left standing," Trixie said. "Well, one, with another as backup."

"I don't want a backup. Why does this have to be so complicated? Last night with Mitchell was amazing. Why'd these other guys have to come along and spoil it?"

"First of all, don't allow the other guys to spoil anything. Take a minute to enjoy the fact that you're a hot ticket around here. Then forget about the other men and focus on Mitchell. I know you're sad about losing Marty's friendship, but you got along fine before you two were friends. Plus, I think he'll eventually decide he'd rather have you as a friend than not at all. And second, I need all the Mitchell details, pronto."

I was about to give her the rundown of our evening when I looked at my watch.

"Holy cow!" I scrambled off the bed. "I'm going to be late for youth group. Gotta run. Thanks for listening."

"You owe me a Mitchell update."

I rushed into the church fellowship hall at 6:53, so I was technically not late for the 7:00 meeting, but I had planned to be there a half hour early.

Greg was chatting with some boys at a table at the far end of the room. He made eye contact and held up a hand in greeting but didn't give me his usual friendly smile. I hoped our friendship was still salvageable, but I knew it might take some time.

"Beckett!" A junior high girl ran up and hugged me.

"Hey, Tiffani. How—"

"Guess what happened at school today. Guess!"

"Aliens landed on the football field?"

Tiffani swatted me on the arm. "No, silly, we had basketball cheerleader tryouts, and I made it! I'm on the eighth-grade squad!" She jumped up and down and pointed at her friend standing shyly off to the side. "Courtney, too!"

"Congratulations, girls!" I pulled Courtney in for a hug. "I'm proud of you both." I was glad Courtney was getting involved in school activities. Her family had moved to Cherry Hill in the spring, and it had taken her a while to work up the courage to make friends.

"I wish we were high school cheerleaders," Tiffani said, "so we could cheer for Cory." She sighed dramatically and Courtney turned red.

"Cory Hankins?" I asked.

"Uh-huh. He's sooooo cute." Tiffani grabbed Courtney's hand and swung it back and forth. "Courtney thinks so, too, but she won't admit it."

"He's also four years older than you," I stated.

"Who cares? What do those high school girls have that I don't have?"

Hopefully a little self-restraint, for starters. But I said, "A few years of life experience. Doesn't Cory have a girlfriend, though?" I probed.

"Yeah." Tiffani frowned. "But she's off at college." She perked back up.

"Kimberly Banner, right?"

She nodded. "Word on the street is she's flunking out, though."

"Do you believe everything you hear 'on the street'?"

"No, but I'm pretty sure it's true she's not going to make it through the semester. Guess she'll have to find a job," she frowned again, "which probably means she'll move back here, though. Dang it."

I held back a laugh at the idea of Tiffani thinking she might have a chance with Cory. I'd been as boy crazy at thirteen as she was, though, so I knew how she felt.

"All right, girls, enough boy talk. We need to get started."

Brrrring!

I dashed across the kitchen to answer the phone.

"Hello?" I said breathlessly.

"Beckett, I'm glad I caught you."

"Hey, Mom." I took a few heavy breaths and dropped into a chair at the kitchen table.

"I've got good news. Wait. What's wrong with you?"

"Phone was ringing when I walked in the door, and I rushed to get it."

"Oh. Anyway, Perry's doing better. He's even conscious for the first time. The doctors can't explain it, but nobody's complaining."

I sighed with relief. "I'm so glad."

"We are, too. He's not out of the woods yet, but this is much better news than earlier today. Anyway, can you call around town and tell whoever would want to know? I don't want to pay long-distance charges from here."

"I'll do it. Tell Perry I say hi, and to get better soon."

"I will, honey. I'll talk to you tomorrow."

My first call was to the police station. As expected, Darren was still there, and he was happy to hear the news.

"Do you know where Aunt Star is?" I had no idea why she wasn't home, especially since Darren was still at work.

"No." He paused. "Obviously you don't either. Where would she be at 8:45 on a Wednesday night?" Darren rarely sounded worried, so his concern made me concerned.

"I don't know. Hang on. Let me see if she left a note."

I stood, surveyed the room, and spotted a piece of note paper on the counter by the sink. I stretched the phone cord across the room and grabbed it.

"Here we go." I read the note aloud. "'Meeting Jacqui for drinks at The Blue Barn. Join us if you want.' Weird. She never hangs out with Jacqui. I wonder how this happened." I hadn't talked to my aunt since lunch.

"I don't know, and I don't like it." Darren now sounded angry.

"Settle down, buddy. They're in a public place. What do you think is going to happen?"

He took such a deep breath I could hear it over the phone.

"Take a few more of those breaths," I ordered. "I'm going to head over there. The two of us will stick together, okay?"

"You be careful, you hear me?"

"Yes, Uncle Darren." I hung up before he could respond, but then I realized I forgot to ask him what he found out about Aggie, if anything. I didn't call back, because I figured he wouldn't tell me anyway.

I was desperate to find out what Aunt Star and Jacqui were talking about at the bar, but I needed to make a few more phone calls about Perry first. I pulled the phone book out of the junk drawer and found Christine's number. She was relieved to hear the news about her boss.

"Do you have Aggie's number?" I asked. "She's too new to

be in the phone book." I could have asked Christine to call her, but I decided I'd rather do it.

"I don't. I'm sure it's written down somewhere at the bank, but I'm not allowed to go there after hours without Perry or Jeff."

"No problem. I'll call the operator. But in case her number is unlisted, do you know where she lives?"

"She's in one of those old apartments over by the fairgrounds. You know the ones?"

"I do." The building held four units and needed a drastic overhaul. "Thanks. Can you call Stan Jones and let him know?"

"Will do."

I dialed the operator and discovered Aggie's number wasn't listed, which was suspicious. Only people with high-profile jobs or who have something to hide didn't list their numbers. Aggie was definitely not high profile.

Next, I called Veronica to tell her the news about Perry. I also quickly filled her in on what I learned from Trixie and the girls at church, and I told her about meeting Aunt Star at The Blue Barn.

"You girls be careful," she said. "Don't do anything stupid."

"We won't. You're welcome to join us."

"If it weren't The Blue Barn, I would."

I found it amusing Veronica defied her husband in numerous ways, but going to The Blue Barn was a line she wouldn't cross.

She continued, "I might call you later to find out what's happening. Don't call me, though, because I don't want Harold getting suspicious."

Chapter Sixteen

The jukebox was blasting "Maneater" when I entered The Blue Barn. I spotted Aunt Star and Jacqui at a table in the back and headed their way. As I passed the bar, a hand reached out in front of me. I came to a halt before running into it and my gaze followed the arm up to Kyle's face.

I didn't have the patience to deal with him at the moment, but I also didn't want to be rude. "Hey, Kyle. What's up?"

He spun on his stool to completely face me and nodded to his side. "Dragged the roommate here to try to cheer him up. He's in a terrible mood tonight."

My face heated when I noticed Marty sitting next to Kyle.

"Hi, Marty," I said tentatively.

He turned his head enough to look in my general direction, give a curt nod, and face the bar again. Kyle raised an eyebrow at the exchange but surprisingly didn't comment.

"Want to join us?" Kyle asked. "Marty'll buy you a drink," he teased.

Marty's body visibly tensed, and my throat tightened.

"I'm meeting Aunt Star." I nodded in her direction. "Thanks, though."

"Anytime." He took a sip of his beer. "Since when are Starla and Jacqui friends?"

"Since never, as far as I know." I smiled at him. "I heard you and Jacqui are, ahem, *friends,* though."

He leaned his back against the bar and grinned at me. "We've been friendly a time or two. Maybe three."

"Hard to keep track, is it?"

He chuckled. "You know how it is. But I found out she was also tangled up with some loser over in Taylorville. I don't need the aggravation of dealing with that kind of situation, so I decided she and I shouldn't be friendly anymore."

"Oh, yeah? Who's the guy?" I asked innocently.

"Sam something-or-other. He's got a funny last name."

"Dalrymple," Marty supplied without turning toward us. "Played football against him in high school." He guzzled down half his beer bottle in one go.

"That's it," Kyle said after giving Marty a shrewd look. "Sam Dalrymple. A real piece of work from what I hear. Lost his job after threatening to shoot a co-worker. Don't know what the woman sees in him. Plenty of other fish in the sea, though." He set his empty bottle on the bar and gave me a lazy smile. "What would happen if I cast my rod at you?"

I laughed at his candor. "It's hard to see how any girl could turn down such a romantic proposition, but I've already been reeled in."

"Have you, now?" He crossed his arms over his chest and smirked at me. "By who?" His expression turned speculative. "By whom? By who. Whom ... who." He shook his head and gave me an expectant look, as if he hadn't just experienced a minor grammatical crisis.

I shot a glance at Marty, who was still facing away from us. "Mitchell Crowe."

"I figured something was going on between you two beyond a casual reunion date, considering how angry he was after he swooped in to keep us from getting killed." Kyle nodded. "The man tried to hide it, but even through my pain I could almost see the smoke coming out of his ears when he marched you out of the room." He gave me a thumbs-up. "Anyway, good for you. He seems like a stand-up guy."

"Thanks. I'd better get over to my aunt."

"Good to see you, Becky. Tell your fisherman I say hi and thanks again for saving my life." He elbowed Marty. "Marty, say goodbye to the pretty lady."

Marty turned slowly on his barstool and pinned me with a steely gaze. "Goodbye, Beckett."

His words sounded so final, my own goodbye caught in my throat. I waved awkwardly and spun away from them.

"Hey, man, what's your deal?" Kyle's voice carried to me as I walked away. I sped up so I wouldn't hear Marty's response.

"Becky," Jacqui said as a greeting when I reached the table.

I pulled out the chair facing away from the bar and practically fell into it.

"What were you talking to Kyle about?" Jacqui asked before I could gather my wits about me.

"My boyfriend," I said without considering whether I wanted her to know about him.

"What boyfriend?"

"Mitchell Crowe. He's a detective."

"I know. Met him when Mom was in jail. No thanks to you."

Suzanne had temporarily been charged with murder in one of the cases earlier in the year.

"That was not my fault," I said. "In fact, her getting out of jail was all down to me finding the real killer."

"Oh, yeah. Sorry. I'm still bitter about the way they treated my mom."

"They had good reason to suspect her," I held up a hand to

stop her retort, "but I know what you're saying. I would feel the same if it were my mom."

A waitress came to take my drink order. Since I hadn't eaten dinner yet, I also ordered a burger and fries to go with my Cherry Coke.

"Speaking of boyfriends," I said to Jacqui, "I hear you're dating someone."

She cut a glance toward Kyle. "Who'd you hear that from?"

"Multiple people, actually, and they will remain unnamed. So tell us about this guy. Is it serious?"

"I'm not going to talk to you about my boyfriend," she said.

I shrugged. "Guess I'll have to believe all the gossip, then."

"What gossip?"

"If you're not talking, I'm not talking."

"Fine. His name is Sam. He lives in Taylorville. He's way more into me than I'm into him." Her eyes flickered toward Kyle again. "I just want to have some fun, but he seems to want more. Hey, I gotta run to the ladies' room. Be back soon."

As soon as she left, Aunt Star asked quietly, "What's wrong? Did Kyle or Marty say something that upset you?"

Tears welled up in my eyes, and I looked at the ceiling to keep them from falling. I was thankful I didn't reapply my eye makeup before youth group. "I can't talk about it here."

"You sure?"

I nodded and swiped my fingers under my eyes. "Why are you here with Jacqui?"

"I ran into her at the IGA after work, and she asked me if I wanted to meet for a drink. I couldn't say no without being rude. Plus, I figured I'd see what she knows about the robbery. When you walked up, she was asking if Darren talks to me about his cases."

"Interesting. Speaking of the robbery ..." I told her what

we had discovered about Aggie and what I'd learned about Sam.

"I remember Sam Dalrymple. He was several years younger than me, but he was the best high school quarterback anybody had seen around here in a long time."

"Star quarterback or not, the man is a criminal and threatened to shoot someone recently."

"That's rather damning."

"Sure is." I was beginning to tell her about Kimberly and Cory when Jacqui returned.

"You talking about Cory Hankins?" Jacqui asked. "What's he done now?"

"How do you know Cory?" I asked in response. Jacqui hadn't been back in Cherry Hill for long, and her only child was in elementary school.

"I don't really know him. I guess you could say I'm friends with his mom. And I hear about him at book club."

"You go to a book club?" I asked.

"Don't look so surprised. I can read, you know, but to be fair, I often don't read the books. I go for the wine and gossip. Anyway, what about Cory?"

"I was telling Aunt Star how all the girls in the youth group are in love with him."

"You would be, too, if you were their age. For that matter, so would I. He's dating that Banner girl, though."

"You mean Kimberly?" I was tired of people calling her "that Banner girl," even if she might be a bank robber.

"There's not another Banner girl, as far as I'm aware," she said testily. "She and Cory have gotten up to some pretty wild stuff."

Aunt Star and I locked gazes.

"Like what?" Aunt Star pressed.

"The usual teenage stuff like stealing road signs,

destroying mailboxes, and harassing campers out at the wildlife area."

I did exactly none of those things as a teenager. I was pretty sure at least one of them was a felony. Apparently Jacqui had a much more colorful adolescent experience than I did. I wouldn't be surprised to find out Jeff had done some of those things, but at least he didn't drag me into it.

She continued in a low voice, "They also stole Coach's checkbook and bought a bunch of stuff using forged checks. They almost cleared out his account. But you didn't hear that from me."

"You're kidding," I said.

"Nope. Part of me wonders if those two robbed the bank."

My eyes flew to Aunt Star's again.

Jacqui pointed between us. "You two wonder the same thing. Don't even try to deny it."

I shrugged. "I won't then."

"So why do you think it might be them, if you didn't already know the stuff I just told you? Or did you only pretend to not know?"

"I didn't know," Aunt Star said.

"Me, neither. Here's what I do know." I couldn't think of a good reason not to tell Jacqui, and I wanted to gauge her response. "Kimberly was seen in town right before the robbery, riding in a car that looks like Missy Hankins' car, with an unidentified man driving. A similar car was seen speeding away from town after the robbery. Cory wasn't in school yesterday morning. Steve and Missy are having some money issues, and Kimberly is about to flunk out of school. She also knows her way around the bank. Add what you told us, and it's hard to not suspect them."

Jacqui listened with interest, but her expression didn't give anything away. "I can see them robbing the bank, but Cory shooting Perry? That's hard to believe."

"I think the guy got spooked. If he really wanted to shoot someone, he would have done it earlier. I don't think shooting anyone was ever part of the plan."

"That's what I'd say, too," Jacqui said. "So who else do you suspect? They can't be the only ones."

I didn't want to tell her about Aggie, because I didn't want that getting around town. And I definitely wasn't telling Jacqui she was a suspect herself.

I hedged, "There might be a few others, but those two seem the most likely." I looked everywhere but at her eyes.

"Hold on a minute. Look me in the eye, Becky Monahan."

I slowly shifted my gaze to hers.

She poked her finger toward me. "You are a terrible liar."

I couldn't deny it, though I hadn't technically lied. Even telling half-truths typically didn't set well with me.

"You suspect me."

I bit my lip.

"I cannot even believe this." Her eyes flashed. "I would cause a scene right here and now, if it wouldn't make me look worse than you already consider me to be. Do you truly believe I would choose to rob my mother and scare the living daylights out of her in the process? I'm ashamed of you. Ashamed."

She stood and shouldered her purse. "You're paying for my drink." Then she stalked out of the bar with her head held high.

"She sure told you," Aunt Star said.

I took a shaky breath. "That's an understatement. At least she didn't scream it." I glanced at the tables around us. Nobody was paying any attention to us, so they hadn't heard a thing.

She continued, "So maybe it wasn't her?"

"I'm not jumping to that conclusion. Think about what she said. She asked if I believe she would choose to rob her

146

mother. Choose. She also didn't say she didn't do it. And she said nothing about me accusing her of robbing an entire bank —just her mom. She was very focused on the Suzanne aspect."

"You're right."

"It could definitely have been her. She might not have even known her mother was in the bank. I'm not sure how she could miss Suzanne's car parked outside, but maybe she was in such a hurry and so focused on the task at hand she didn't see it when they went in. The robbers didn't know anyone was in the room when they arrived, and they didn't know who was in there until the guy forced his way in. The female robber didn't even go in there until after the guy shot Perry. Then she *had* to take what was in the box. If it was Jacqui, and she didn't take the stuff, that would have given her up right then and there."

"And we believe Suzanne wouldn't recognize her daughter, even with the disguise?"

"Suzanne was scared out of her wits. She told us so. She probably didn't even get a good look at the woman, and they were in the same room together for what—twenty seconds, at the most?"

The waitress brought my food, and we sat in silence for a few minutes while I ate.

"Oh!" I said. "I forgot to tell you Perry is better."

"Ah, that's good to hear," she said pleasantly.

I was annoyed by her lackadaisical response until I realized she likely didn't know about his bad turn earlier. "Yeeeeah, I forgot to tell you."

"Forgot to tell me what?" She plucked a fry from my plate and popped it into her mouth.

I told her about the phone call from Pastor Coker about Perry earlier in the day.

"Oh! Well, that's great news now, isn't it? I'm so glad. I bet

Jeff will sleep much easier tonight." She raised an eyebrow. "You still not going to tell me what happened with him this morning?"

"Nope."

"Suit yourself." She tapped her pointer finger on the table. "What about why you looked like you were going to cry when you got here?"

"Not now." Tears welled up again. "I'll tell you when we get home. I promise."

She patted my hand. "Okay. Finish your food. I'll go pay and meet you at the door in a minute. You take care of the tip."

"Don't leave without me," I said around a fry. "Darren wants us to stick together."

"That man—"

I interrupted her, "Worries about you just like he worries about me. Actually more, I'm hoping." I grinned at her.

She rolled her eyes and headed toward the cash register at the far end of the bar. I scarfed down the rest of my fries and pulled a few dollars out of my wallet to leave for the waitress. When I turned around, Marty was still at the bar, but Kyle had gone. Tables full of customers blocked all my other paths, so I couldn't avoid walking by him to leave the building.

I steeled myself as I passed behind Marty. He didn't turn or acknowledge me, and I clenched my fists in frustration.

"Beckett, wait."

Chapter Seventeen

I stopped but didn't turn toward Marty. I caught my aunt's eye where she stood waiting by the door, and she raised her eyebrows at me.

"Please." Marty's tone was desperate.

I unclenched my hands and slowly spun to face him. The hard look from earlier was replaced with sadness. He patted the barstool beside him, and I climbed onto it.

He looked directly into my eyes. "I'm sorry."

My gaze held his. "I know."

He gave me a half smile. "You always think the best of people, don't you?"

Jacqui would beg to differ. So should he, to be accurate.

"Unless I'm suspecting them of armed robbery or murder."

He snorted. "Thanks for the reminder."

"That make you feel better?" I teased.

"It kinda does." One corner of his mouth tipped up.

"Glad I could help."

"I can't believe I treated you the way I did earlier. And that Kyle of all people called me out on it."

"He's full of surprises."

"Speaking of Kyle, you wouldn't ever ...?"

"Not if he were the last living being in the universe. I'd prefer to roll in poison ivy."

He laughed. I knew he wanted to ask the same question about himself, but I also knew he respected me enough not to. Even if he did, I wouldn't answer, as it wouldn't be fair to either of us ... or to Mitchell.

"Jacqui shouldn't be dating Sam," he said, seemingly out of the blue.

"Why do you say that?"

"First, Kyle really likes her. He was pretty upset when he found out about Sam. I think he may finally be getting over my sister—ten years later. And second, Sam is a jerk and always has been."

"Did you know him well in high school?"

"Well enough. I dated his sister for a couple months, which was a mistake."

I felt he had more to say but probably didn't want to speak badly about either of them any more than he already had, so I prompted him, "Care to share why?"

"A few weeks in, I found out she was taking drugs, and Sam was supplying them. I thought I could get her to stop. I was wrong. Sam had this weird control over her. Once I realized she would always do what he wanted her to, we broke up."

"I'm sorry," I said.

"I'm not. She was obviously not the right girl for me."

We were both silent for a moment after that declaration.

"Marty, why didn't you tell me?" I asked softly.

He didn't need to ask what I was talking about. "I was scared."

His vulnerability surprised me, as did the statement itself. "Why?"

"You've turned down everybody who asked you out since

you came back to town. You didn't date at all except for your reunion date with the detective. I didn't think I had a chance until you held my hand yesterday."

I winced at his words. I'd been right about the catalyst for the situation we found ourselves in.

He continued, "I was afraid I'd ruin our friendship if I told you how I felt."

"Does it have to be ruined now?"

He looked away from me. "We'll see."

I slid off my stool onto my feet.

He turned to face me. "I think I'll get there. I need some time."

I touched his arm, but I snatched my hand back when an electric jolt ran up my own arm. The flash in Marty's eyes revealed he felt it, too. My neck and face bloomed red, and he clenched his jaw.

"Sorry," I muttered. "I'll see you later."

"Yeah," he whispered and turned back toward the bar.

I hurried toward the door while inwardly cursing myself. I vowed to never touch another man again unless I was actively dating him or married to him.

"What was that about?" Aunt Star hissed when I reached her.

I towed her out the door with my still-tingling hand. "I'll tell you later."

"You'd better." She pulled her arm out of my grasp when we were several steps down the sidewalk. "Are we allowed to drive home separately, or will that not fulfill Darren's orders?"

I huffed out a breath. "Don't get snippy with me. I can't deal with it right now."

She pulled me into a side hug as we continued down the street. "I'm sorry. What do you want to do—drive together or on our own?"

"Together. You can drive. I parked in the church lot, so my

car will be fine there overnight. We need to make a stop before going home, though." I still needed to stop by Aggie's house to tell her about Perry. If she wasn't the robber, and I was starting to think she wasn't, she deserved to know about him, even if she had lied on her job application.

"All right," my aunt said. "I'm parked the other way, though."

We turned and headed back in the direction of the bar. The door opened as we approached it, and Marty stepped out. We locked eyes, and my feet stopped moving, as did his. Aunt Star continued walking until she realized she was alone. She turned and looked back and forth between Marty and me.

"Marty," she said carefully, "you doing all right tonight?"

His gaze snapped to her, and I let out the breath I'd been holding.

"I've been better, but I'll live. You?"

"Considering we're being honest here, I'm rather confused at the moment, but I'm hoping my niece will help me out with that."

He nodded once, stuffed his hands into his pockets, and made his way down the sidewalk without another word. I was tempted to tell him not to walk with his hands in his pockets, but I restrained myself.

Aunt Star took me by the elbow and marched me down the sidewalk. "Beckett Lee Monahan, you have a lot of explaining to do. I could have cut that tension with a butter knife."

We got into the car, and she started the engine and cranked up the heat, but she didn't touch the gearshift.

"I don't know where you think we still need to go at this time of night, but we're not going anywhere until you tell me what's going on between you and Marty James."

I burst into tears for what I prayed would be the final time of the day.

Aunt Star turned to me from the driver's seat. "You sure you're up for this after the day you've had?"

I stared at the apartment building in front of us. The parking spot designated for apartment three held a car I recognized as a regular in the bank parking lot, so there was no question which door was Aggie's. Light filtered around the curtains at the front window of her apartment.

"Might as well get it over with," I said.

"I'm coming with you."

"You bet you are."

"Darren and Mitchell will kill us both for doing this ... if Aggie doesn't kill us first."

"She's not going to kill us. Let's go."

Aunt Star trailed me up the sidewalk, and I rapped on the door. Within seconds, the light went out, but nobody came to the door. I knocked again.

"Maybe say who it is," my aunt said. "I'm not sure I would answer the door at this time of night if I didn't expect a visitor."

"Aggie, it's Beckett Monahan," I said loudly, but I hoped not loudly enough to annoy the neighbors. "I'm here about Perry Adamson."

A light scraping sounded from the other side of the door, the lock clicked, and the door jerked open, revealing a wide-eyed, wild-haired Aggie standing in the dark in a long, plaid flannel nightgown. She held one hand behind her back and the other rested on her stomach.

"He's dead, isn't he?" She looked stricken.

I could only imagine the state my face was in after my latest round of crying, which would make her fear the worst, but I was surprised by the depth of her emotion.

"No. Instead of getting worse, he got better. He was even conscious this evening for the first time."

She closed her eyes and moved her hand to rest over her heart. "Oh, thank goodness."

I didn't know whether she was relieved because she cared about him or because her partner in crime now wouldn't be charged with murder, but I was determined to find out.

"Aggie, where did you work before you came to Cherry Hill?"

Aunt Star tugged backward on my elbow, but I stood firm.

Aggie chewed her lip. "Um, Battlefield Savings Bank in Springfield."

"Then why have they never heard of you?"

Terror filled her eyes. "That's none of your business." She slammed the door in my face, and the lock clicked.

Aunt Star hauled me back to her car. Before I was fully settled into my seat, she peeled out of the parking lot.

"That woman had a gun," she declared.

"She did not!"

"Then why was one hand behind her back the entire time? That's weird. Nobody stands like that. She had a gun!"

"Oh."

"We're telling Darren."

"All right. We'll call him when we get home."

"We are going to the police station. If he's not there, we'll go to his house." She took a corner so quickly I grabbed the door handle to stay upright.

"Why are you all fired up about this?" I had rarely seen her so worked up about anything.

"Because that woman had a gun!" She slammed her hand against the steering wheel. "Do you not understand what I'm saying? She could have shot us!"

"But she didn't."

"Becks, maybe you've been held at gunpoint before, but I

have not. And I never want to be. Plus, she's obviously the bank robber. Why else would she be holding a gun when she answered the door?"

"I don't know."

The lobby lights were dimmed at the police station, but several cars were parked outside. Aunt Star pounded on the door while I calmly pressed the doorbell next to the sign that said, "Ring here after 9:00 pm."

Frank crossed the darkened lobby and opened the door but didn't step aside. "How can I help you ladies?"

My aunt shouldered him out of her way and marched into the building. "I need to talk to my boyfriend, if you don't mind, Frank Nichols."

"What's she all riled up about?" Frank whispered to me.

"You'll hear about it soon enough, I'm sure."

I scurried along in her wake across the pit and into Darren's office. She slammed the door behind me.

"That woman has a gun." She pointed toward the front of the building.

Darren jumped to his feet and yanked his gun out of its holster before I could register what was happening.

"Where? Who? Outside?" He gently but firmly pushed us out of the way to get to the door.

"Stop!" Aunt Star ordered.

Amazingly, Darren froze in place.

"The lady with the gun isn't here."

He closed his eyes and pressed his lips together. "Where is she?" He asked through gritted teeth. "Who is she?" He finally opened his eyes. "Jacqui, I presume?"

My aunt put her hands on her hips. "No, why would you think that?"

Darren's eyes closed again. "Starla Beckett, I swear to—"

I cut him off before he could say something he would undoubtedly regret. "Aggie Goldsby has a gun. Well, Aunt Star thinks she does. We didn't see it. Oh, and she's at her apartment."

Darren put his gun back where it belonged and sank into his chair.

"Sit down. Both of you."

I sat. His girlfriend did not.

"Starla," his voice was calm yet commanding, "don't make me tell you again. This is not one of our spats. We are not in my living room. This is my office. This is a police matter. You will sit in that chair, and you will tell me what is going on *right now.*"

My aunt glared at him, but she sat. I was more than a little disappointed I wasn't going to find out what would happen if she refused. I was also quite curious about the living room spats he referred to.

"Beckett."

I jerked to attention. "Yes?"

"Did I or did I not tell you to be careful?"

"You did."

"And?"

"I was. And then I wasn't, but only a little bit. We did stick together, though, just like I promised." I gave him my sunniest smile in an attempt to counteract the eye daggers Aunt Star was flinging at him.

Darren took a deep breath in through his nose and looked at the ceiling. I could almost hear him counting to ten in his head. Then he lowered his chin and looked me in the eye. "Tell me what happened tonight. And this time, give me the most pertinent details first. I don't need to know what you drank at the bar or who else was there or what they were wearing."

It was my turn to glare at him. "That was uncalled for. I don't have to tell you anything, unless I'm under arrest. Am I under arrest?"

Aunt Star reached over and grabbed my hand in solidarity.

Darren sighed, and his eyes and voice lost their hard edge. "I'm sorry, okay? To both of you. It's been a long two days, and I'm well past being on my last nerve. Please, for the love of all things holy, tell me what's going on here. I don't care how you do it. Just tell me what I need to know."

My aunt squeezed my hand, which I took as her approval for me to talk, since she didn't speak up.

"We talked to Jacqui at The Blue Barn. Wait. First, I talked to Kyle."

"Beck—" Darren clamped his mouth shut.

"It's pertinent, I promise. Kyle told me Sam Dalrymple lost his job because he threatened to shoot a co-worker."

Darren uncapped a pen and started writing notes. I told him what I learned from Veronica about Sam, and I relayed our conversation with Jacqui and my theory about how she still could have been involved.

"Where does Aggie Goldsby and an invisible gun come into play?" Darren asked.

"It wasn't invisible!" Aunt Star said. "I just couldn't see it!"

"Okay, I hear you," Darren said. "I *do*," he insisted after what I assumed was another glare from my aunt.

I explained why we went to Aggie's house and what was said.

"As Aunt Star pointed out to me, she did keep one hand behind her back the whole time," I said. "Maybe she had a gun. Maybe she didn't. Here's the thing, though. When I asked why nobody at the other bank had heard of her, she looked absolutely terrified. If she thought the other bank not knowing her could tip us off about her being the person who robbed our bank, I would expect her to be angry or to act nervous or shifty. Maybe she would have even pulled the gun on us. Instead she had a look of sheer terror."

"Now that you mention it, she did," my aunt agreed. "And did you hear the scraping sound before she opened the door?"

"I did."

"I think a chair was shoved under the doorknob to help keep someone from busting in. She had no idea we were coming, but she thought someone might come, and she was scared."

A knock sounded on the door, and I jumped a mile.

"What?" Darren barked.

Frank popped his head in. "Boss, Aggie Goldsby is on the phone. Says she has something to tell us."

Aunt Star and I looked at each other with wide eyes.

"Tell her to come in," Darren said to Frank.

"I did. She wants a police escort. Can we do that?"

"What did we tell you?" Aunt Star said. "She's terrified of something—or somebody."

"Go pick her up," Darren said to Frank. "Take Jake with you."

"No, take me," I said. "A terrified woman does not need to be alone in a car with two male police officers. No offense, Frank."

"None taken."

Darren shook his head. "I can't let you do that. We don't know what Frank and Jake are going to face when they get there. If Aggie has a gun, and this is a setup," he pointed at me, "I don't want you anywhere near there. Actually, I should go, too." He stood and looked at Aunt Star and me in turn. "You two stay here. Don't you dare leave until we know what's going on out there. You're safest here."

We nodded silently.

"All right, Frank, let's go."

Chapter Eighteen

Darren took a step toward the open office door, but Aunt Star jumped up and blocked his path. He gave her a wary look. Instead of yelling at him like he and I expected, she wrapped her arms around him, and he reciprocated.

"Be careful," she mumbled into his chest.

"I will." He clasped her shoulders and pushed her slightly away from him. Then he tipped her chin up so he could look her in the eyes. "I know you're scared, babe. But I have a gun, too, as do Frank and Jake. We'll be fine."

He leaned down and gave her a lingering kiss and then moved her back into the chair before closing the door behind him. Darren didn't do public displays of affection, so kissing my aunt like that in front of me and whoever might be watching from the pit revealed how much he cared for her.

Aunt Star reached out and gripped my hand again.

"He kissed you in public—well, semi-public," I said. "Let's take a moment for that to sink in."

She squeezed my hand. "I don't like it. I mean, I *liked* it, but it was so out of character it scares me even more. I don't want to think about him and guns and what's happening out

159

there, so let's talk about your man situation. What in the world are you going to do?"

"I have no idea. At least I don't have to figure out what I'm going to say to Mitchell tonight—if there's anything I need to say at all. It's too late to talk to him on the phone now."

"What do you want to do, though? Do you want to see where things lead with Mitchell or with Marty?"

"If I end things with Mitchell, that'll probably be it. I don't think there will be any going back. But if I stick with Mitchell for now, there still may be a chance with Marty in the future if things don't work out with Mitchell."

"That's the practical way of looking at it, but I think you need to let your heart lead you on this, not your head."

"The problem is I think my heart might want both of them."

"That's a significant problem. I don't know what to tell you, kiddo."

"Do you think Darren meant we can't leave this office, or can we just not leave the station?" I asked. "Because I really need to use the restroom."

"I'm going to make a *de facto* decision and approve your request."

I squeezed her hand. "You'll be okay here by yourself?"

"Yeah. Stop by the break room on your way back and grab me a cup of water, will you?"

"Sure."

When I approached Darren's office carrying two cups of water a few minutes later, a man was talking to Aunt Star. As I got closer, I recognized the voice. I stopped walking so quickly that water sloshed out of the cups. I hadn't thought I would talk to Mitchell that evening, much less see him. My heart began to race.

The one officer still left in the pit raised an eyebrow at me. I gave him a fake smile and stepped forward. My foot slipped on the spilled water, and I shrieked and skidded forward. My shoulder banged against the doorframe of Darren's office, and the water cups went flying.

Mitchell caught me before I hit the ground. Then he hauled me back up to my feet and pulled me close. I slipped my hands around his waist to hold him tightly, and he pressed his lips to my temple. When I turned my face up to his, his gaze focused on my lips before moving to my eyes.

I couldn't help but think about the almost identical situation I had found myself in with another man ten hours earlier. Tears pricked behind my eyelids as I wished I had gone straight back to work after lunch instead of to the hardware store. I could've saved myself a lot of heartache.

He swept a thumb across my cheek to wipe away the lone tear that escaped. "What's wrong?"

I took a shaky breath and said, "I'm fine. It's been a long day."

He gave me an intense look before quickly pressing his lips to mine and sliding a hand down to my own. He led me to Darren's chair and then stuck his head back out the office door to ask the officer in the pit if he would clean up the water.

While Mitchell wasn't looking, Aunt Star looked at me with wide eyes. With my own eyes, I implored her not to leave Mitchell and me alone together. I couldn't deal with a private conversation with him at the moment. She gave me a nod of acknowledgement.

Mitchell closed the door and took the seat I had vacated minutes earlier. He looked at me but tipped his head toward my aunt. "Starla was telling me what's happening. Sounds like they should be back here soon?"

I nodded. "I thought you weren't coming until tomorrow." He was wearing jeans and a tight-fitting black T-shirt, so I didn't think he intended to be working. My eyes roamed up and down his torso, admiring his muscle definition, before I focused on his face again. He smirked to let me know he noticed what I was doing, and I looked away from him as my face flushed.

"Darren called this evening to tell me all that transpired during the day, and I decided to pack my bags and drive on over here tonight so I'd be ready to dive in at the crack of dawn. When I drove by here on my way to The Osh, I saw Starla's car outside but didn't think much of it. Then I saw your car in the church lot, but no lights seemed to be on inside the church, so I came back here to see what was going on."

Movement in the pit caught my eye, and I peered through the window while Mitchell and Aunt Star turned to see what I was looking at. In the larger room, Jake returned to his desk, while Darren and Frank led Aggie toward an interview room. Her shoulders sagged, she pressed one hand to her stomach, and she focused on the floor the entire time.

Mitchell stood and opened the door. "Turley."

Darren swiveled toward him, turned back to say something to Frank, and then made his way over to us. Frank continued to the interview room with Aggie, while Aunt Star and I crowded behind Mitchell. We couldn't see around him, so we both stood on our tiptoes to peek over his shoulders.

"Ladies," Darren said, "back up and give the man some space."

Mitchell glanced over his shoulder and smiled at me. Then he turned and herded us back into the office.

Darren followed him in and shut the door. "Detective Crowe, do you want to sit in on this interview?"

"I wouldn't want to miss it."

"Good. Ladies, I need you to go home. Officer Park will follow you to make sure you arrive safely."

"But—"

"No buts, Beckett. This might take a while. We'll call if there's anything you need to know." Darren put his hand on the doorknob.

"You're not going to tell us what happened at her house?" I asked.

"We knocked, she opened the door, got in the car, and here we are. She hasn't said a word."

"Ask her if she's pregnant," Aunt Star suggested.

Everyone's gaze snapped to her.

"Why?" Mitchell asked.

"Both times we've seen her tonight, she had her hand on her belly the way pregnant women do." She demonstrated. "I'm surprised Minda and Christine didn't notice that at the bank."

If Aggie was pregnant, I couldn't imagine she would put herself and the baby in danger by robbing the bank. It was looking more and more like she wasn't the culprit, but something fishy was going on.

Darren nodded, but before he opened the door he said, "Beckett, will you see if you can track down Jeff? Tell him Aggie may or may not show up for work tomorrow. Regardless, he should talk to me before talking to her."

"I'll find him," I said while avoiding Mitchell's gaze.

Darren left the office, and Aunt Star followed. Mitchell stepped between me and the doorway and trailed his fingers down my arms before holding my hands loosely in his. "You're not yourself tonight, and you've been crying. You're obviously not fine." He cocked his head to the side. "What's going on?"

I bit my lip. "I'm just exhausted. We'll talk tomorrow."

His eyes revealed he didn't believe my excuse. He lightly pressed his lips to my forehead, and my heart dropped when he let go of my hands and turned away from me. I grasped his arm, turned him back around, and pulled his head down to meet mine. He initially didn't respond to my kiss, but I persisted, and he finally gave in, albeit briefly. His eyes searched mine again before he left. I stood in a daze until Aunt Star grabbed my arm and pulled me through the pit.

Jake followed us out the front door, and Aunt Star turned to him before we got in her car. "We need to make a stop at First Community Church to pick up Beckett's car." She looked at me. "You're okay to drive, right?"

I nodded and slid into the passenger seat without a word.

"You have to get this mess figured out tonight," she said as she cranked the engine. "Mitchell knows something's wrong. You can't pull one over on a detective."

"I know."

We rode to the church in silence. Jake dutifully followed us all the way home and waited until we were safely inside the house before leaving.

I flipped through the phone book to the J's and dialed Jeff's number on the kitchen phone.

"This is Jeff."

I dropped into a kitchen chair. "This is Beckett. I hope I didn't wake you."

"No. We got home about a half hour ago but I'm not in bed yet."

"How's Perry?"

"Doing better. He even said a few words to me before I left."

"I'm so glad to hear that."

"Yep."

"I'm calling to give you the latest on Aggie." I filled him in on the details.

"Wow. I'll admit I'm intrigued."

"Me, too. What time are you opening the bank in the morning?"

"Seven o'clock."

"You better get to sleep. If I hear anything about Aggie later tonight, I'll give you a call in the morning."

"If I can drag myself out of bed early enough, I may drop by the station before work to see what they know."

"Sounds good. I'll talk to you tomorrow."

"Night, Becky. Thanks again for everything today."

"You're most welcome. Good night."

When I reached the top of the stairs, Aunt Star called out to me from her room. I headed down the hall, kicked my shoes off, and crawled into her bed fully clothed. She shook her head at me but didn't order me out. A few minutes later she was in her pajamas and curled up facing me.

She put her hand on my cheek in an uncharacteristic display of affection. "I love you, Becks."

I gave her a wobbly smile and put my hand on top of her own. "Love you, too."

She pulled her hand away and slipped it under her pillow. "Let's figure this out. Together."

I nodded.

"What was your first reaction when you realized Mitchell was at the station?"

"Dread."

Her eyebrows shot up. "Really?"

"I didn't want to talk to him—not tonight, not with my emotions so raw."

"Did you dread touching him?"

"Not at all. I wanted him to touch me, to kiss me."

"That's a good sign."

"But I couldn't help thinking about Marty when Mitchell held me after I almost fell."

"What about when you kissed him? Who did you think about then?"

"Only him."

"Him meaning Mitchell," she clarified.

"Uh-huh."

She tucked a curl behind my ear. "You obviously care about both of these men."

"I'm a terrible person."

"You are not."

"How can I have feelings for two men at the same time? It's wrong!"

"It's not. It happens to the best of us, believe me." I did believe her. She dated both Darren and Aidan for a short time early in the year. "But you need to make a choice," she said. "You have to overcome your feelings for one of them."

Her advice sounded exactly like what I told Greg earlier in the day.

She grinned at me. "Something tells me neither of them will want to share you."

I chuckled. "Can you imagine? I don't want that either. One man is enough."

"Let's think about this from a different angle. If you have to let one of them go—and you do—which one will you be most upset to lose?"

I closed my eyes as I thought about my answer.

"Did you fall asleep?" Aunt Star whispered.

"No, I'm thinking."

"Tell me your thoughts."

I didn't open my eyes. "If we were only talking friendship, I'd say Marty."

"But we're not just talking friendship. We're talking the whole package."

"I've never dated Marty, so I don't know how I would feel if I didn't have that anymore."

"Do you want to lose Mitchell?"

My eyes popped open. "No."

Aunt Star didn't respond. She knew she couldn't make the final decision for me.

"It's Mitchell. I want Mitchell."

"There you go. Stick with him." She leaned over and kissed my cheek. "Now go to sleep."

"But what do I do about Marty? I can't leave him hanging —not after tonight."

"There will be plenty of time to think about that tomorrow." She rolled over and switched off the bedside lamp.

"Do you think Darren will call to update us about Aggie?" I asked into the darkness.

"What do you think?"

I didn't need to see her eyes to know she was rolling them.

I poked her back. "When are you going to make him my uncle?"

"Go to sleep, Becks."

"I need some little baby cousins."

She fake snored.

I smiled into the darkness and prayed for sleep to come quickly.

Chapter Nineteen

A beeping alarm woke me with a start. The room was dark, and my leg was touching another body. I shrieked and flailed my legs. "Who's there? Where am I?"

The other person groaned and a few seconds later the beeping stopped.

"You're in my bed," Aunt Star said sleepily. "Stop kicking me, get out, and go brush your teeth. Your breath smells like a tuna factory."

"Sor-ry, Miss Grumpy Pants." I swept my tongue across my teeth and almost gagged at the fuzzy texture. She had a point. "I forgot to brush my teeth last night."

She pushed my arm. "Out. Stop talking."

"What time is it?"

"Six o'clock. Go!" She pushed me again.

"Ugh. Why do you get up so early?"

"I just do. Get out of my bed."

"I'm going. I'm going." I stumbled out of her room and down the hall to my bathroom. I didn't like the view in the mirror. My hair was ratted, my eyes were puffy, and my neck was covered with jagged creases from the collar of the shirt I'd been wearing since the previous evening.

I wanted to go back to bed and sleep for another hour, but I wanted fresh breath and a shower even more. I turned on the bath tap and then brushed my teeth while waiting for the warm water to make its way from the basement.

Forty minutes later I was dressed in a burnt orange button-up dress and burgundy flats and had corralled my drying curls into a scrunchie. I opted against wearing eye makeup, considering I would likely have some emotional conversations during the day.

The smell of coffee greeted me as I descended the stairs. Aunt Star handed me a full cup when I entered the kitchen. "Drink up. Darren called while you were in the shower. He wants us to come to the station."

"Did he even sleep?" I took a gulp of coffee and grabbed a granola bar out of the pantry.

"I doubt it."

"Did he say what he's going to tell us?"

"If he did, we wouldn't need to go down there, would we?"

"Don't test me," I said around a bite of granola bar. "I can't waste my emotional energy on you today. I need to save it for my men."

She gave me a sharp look. "You're going to get yourself in trouble if you refer to them that way, even in jest. Only one of them is your man." She drained her coffee cup and set it in the sink. "You still set on which one that is?"

"Yep."

"All righty then. Time to face the music." She opened the door into the garage but slammed it back shut. "Holy moly it turned frigid overnight. Get your coat and gloves. I hope you're wearing your thickest pantyhose."

"I need your official statement about your conversations with and about Jacqui, Sam, Cory, and Kimberly yesterday. I'll be recording this and taking notes."

Darren sat across from me in one of the two interview rooms. Aunt Star was with Mitchell in the room next door. I assumed they were doing the same thing, but I wasn't sure, because Darren had whisked me inside before I could do little more than glance at Mitchell.

"That's going to take a while."

"I know. Don't editorialize. Just give me the facts."

He looked haggard after what I assumed was a sleepless night, so I didn't argue with him.

"Wait," I said. "You didn't mention Aggie's name."

"I did not."

"Why?"

"I'll tell you when we're done with the other."

"Why?"

"Because that will give you incentive to hurry this up." He hit the record button on the tape recorder and stated the date, time, and our names. "Go."

I relayed every piece of information I could remember. Then he stopped the recording.

"Now about Aggie," Darren said. "Normally I wouldn't tell you all of this, but she asked me to."

"Really? Why?"

"She likes you, and she's afraid you think the worst of her. She wants you to know the truth, but she was too nervous to tell you herself. I told her you would understand, but she was adamant it be me."

"Ooookay. I take it she wasn't the bank robber?"

"No, but she may well be connected, through no fault of her own. Aggie did work at Battlefield Savings Bank, but her real name is Margaret Silverton."

"Margaret ... Maggie ... Aggie," I mused. "And Goldsby instead of Silverton. Clever. Why did she change her name?"

"For protection. She didn't legally change it, but she told everyone here her new name. The only people who knew the truth were Perry and Sandra."

"The Adamsons! Why? How?"

"Aggie and Perry are distant cousins."

I shook my head. "I don't understand."

"If you'll stop interrupting me, I'll tell you the entire story."

"Sorry." I mimed zipping my lips closed.

"Aggie was in an abusive relationship with a career criminal. He pushed her to get the job at the bank in Springfield, and then he tried to get her to steal money from the bank. When she refused, he became violent."

I pressed my hand to my chest but kept silent.

Darren continued, "She's been estranged from her immediate family for a while, but she had fond memories of Perry and his family from her childhood, so she tracked him down and called him for help when she was at the end of her rope. Of course, he helped her." He spread his hands. "You know Perry. He gave her the job, he got her the apartment, and he helped create a new life for her here."

Everything Darren was saying lined up with what I knew about Perry's big heart.

"The last couple weeks, though," he said, "she has felt like someone was watching her—following her. She was afraid it was her ex. She thinks he's the one who robbed the bank and shot Perry."

"And he just happened to do it on the one day she wasn't there?"

"You can't always predict morning sickness."

My eyes widened. "Ohhhh. So she *is* pregnant."

"Yep."

"With the bad guy's baby?"

"Unfortunately."

"Does he know?"

"She doesn't think so."

I tilted my head. "So does she have a boyfriend?"

"No, she said she did to keep men away from her. She didn't want anyone bothering her."

"I hear that," I muttered.

He narrowed his eyes at me. "What did you say?"

"Nothing. You're sure this is all true?"

Darren nodded. "We've confirmed it with Sandra."

"Why didn't Sandra say anything to you about it after the robbery?"

"We never talked to her. She wasn't there when it happened, and she's been at the hospital ever since. She had no idea we suspected Aggie. Jeff didn't mention his suspicions to Sandra, either."

"Will Perry get in trouble for helping her pretend to be someone else?" I asked. "For hiring someone with a fake name?"

"I doubt it. He used her real name on all the official paper-work," he explained. "It's in a file locked in a drawer in his office. He personally handed over her paychecks so nobody would see the name."

"No wonder Aggie was a mess about Perry getting shot and almost dying. She really does care about him, and she would be in a world of hurt without him. No pun intended. Will she get in trouble for using a fake name?"

"She didn't use the fake name on anything legal, so no. And we're working on getting her more protection from her ex."

I nodded. "Good. Can I go see her?"

"I'm sure she'd appreciate that. She's not at work today. Jeff said he was going to tell her to take the day off."

"You've talked to him?"

"He left here right before you arrived. We didn't tell Aggie he suspected her of anything, and we don't intend to let word of that get out. He feels terrible about it, and he doesn't want her to feel uncomfortable working with him going forward."

"So Aggie thinks her ex is the robber, but you must not think so, or you wouldn't be asking me about the others again."

"We're keeping our options open. And we're extremely thankful this hasn't turned into a murder investigation."

"Me, too."

He gave me a speculative look.

"Why are you looking at me like that?"

"Is everything okay with you? You acted strangely last night in my office after Mitchell arrived. And you had obviously been crying."

I pursed my lips. Why was I surrounded by perceptive policemen?

"He didn't do anything deserving of a punch in the nose, did he?" Darren demanded.

I gave him a weak smile. "No. He hasn't done anything wrong." My gaze skittered away from his.

"You sure?" He moved his head to my line of vision.

"Yes." I was the one who messed up. "Do you need anything else from me?"

"One more thing." He paused.

"Yes?" I prompted.

"Why do you keep alluding to your aunt and me getting married?"

"Because I want you to."

"That's all?"

"Yes."

"She hasn't said anything?"

I shook my head.

"Oh." His face fell.

"Don't read anything into that, though. She doesn't often share her feelings about men with me."

"I thought you two told each other everything."

"I tell her almost everything, but she doesn't always return the favor."

"Does she want to get married, though? In general, I mean."

I was surprised they hadn't talked about it. "I'm not in a position to answer that."

"You're right. Forget I asked." He cleared his throat. "I'd better let you get to work."

I reached across the table and put my hand on his. "I will say I have never seen her as comfortable with any man as she is with you. And she has never worried about anyone like she worries about you. You two have something special. In my opinion, if she were to ever decide to marry someone, it would be you."

"I appreciate you saying that." He flipped his hand over, squeezed mine, and stood.

When we left the room, Mitchell was nowhere to be seen, and Aunt Star was sitting in Darren's desk chair. He crossed the room in a few long strides, picked her up out of the chair as if she weighed nothing, kissed her, and set her on her feet. Then he dropped down into the chair.

Her hand shot to her lips. "What was that for?"

"I felt like it," he said.

I grinned at him from his office doorway. His lips twitched, but he didn't smile back.

She shot a "what is happening here" look at me. "Okay."

"You ladies are free to go," Darren said in a casual tone.

"Where's Mitchell?" I wasn't fully prepared to talk to him yet, but I also didn't want to leave without saying goodbye.

"He and Frank went to follow up a lead," Aunt Star explained. "He said to tell you he'll see you later."

"Oh." I was both relieved by the delay and dismayed he left without talking to me.

We said goodbye to Darren, pulled on our coats and gloves, and headed out of the station.

"You want to grab some breakfast at The Check?" I asked my aunt. "Or do you need to get to work? I don't have to be at work for another forty-five minutes."

"You already ate a granola bar."

"This would be more of a social event than an eating event. Come on. Don't make me go alone. Who knows how many men might try to ask me for a date?"

She laughed. "I think you've exhausted the local supply, but sure, I'll go. I don't have any appointments this morning, so I can be late."

Three minutes later we were sitting across from each other in a booth in the front window of The Check.

"What can I get you fine ladies on this chilly morning?" Callie asked, coffee pot in hand.

"Coffee, please." Aunt Star flipped her upturned cup over on the saucer. "And I'll take some scrambled eggs."

"Coffee and two pancakes for me." My granola bar was a distant memory.

Callie filled both of our cups. "Let me put your order in and I'll be right back."

Most of the breakfast crowd had already left for work, so the diner was almost empty. Callie checked out the only remaining customers and slid in next to Aunt Star.

"What's the latest on the investigation? I hear Perry's doing better."

"He sure is." I smiled.

"Also heard the police took Aggie away last night but then

they brought her back a few hours later. Do you know what happened?"

"Mitchell wouldn't tell me." Aunt Star nodded toward me. "Did Darren tell you?"

"He did, but I can't pass it on. It's not my story to tell. But Aggie wasn't involved in the robbery."

"Okay, but why did you," Callie pointed to me, "talk to Darren, while you," she pointed to my aunt, "talked to Mitchell? Did I miss some weird man swapping thing here?"

I laughed. "No. They asked us to come in this morning to tell them everything we know about the current suspects. I guess they thought it wasn't a good idea for them to take the statements from their own girlfriends."

"So who are the current suspects?" Callie asked.

"We've got Jacqui Storm and her boyfriend Sam Dalrymple, as well as Cory Hankins and Kimberly Banner. Oh, and Aggie's ex-boyfriend from Springfield."

"Sam Dalrymple from Taylorville?" Callie said. "Jacqui is dating him? I thought she was with Kyle. Anyway, Sam's a disaster. He was in here last week. Tried to hit on me even though there was a woman with him—who was not Jacqui, by the way—but I shut that down real fast."

I sat up straight. "He was here last week?"

"Yeah, why?"

"Where did he sit?"

"Exactly where you're sitting. Again, why?"

I pointed out the window. They both craned their necks to look and then turned back to me with wide eyes. I had a perfect view of the front of the bank.

A bell dinged near the back of the diner, and Callie jumped up to grab our plates.

"Jacqui wasn't involved in the robbery, though," Callie said when she returned.

I picked up my knife. "How do you know?"

"Because when I got back over here after leaving you all in front of the bank, she was here."

"Here? At The Check?" I waved the knife around in a circle.

"Where else would 'here' be?" Aunt Star asked.

I shot her a glare. "Maybe she was returning to the scene of the crime." I buttered my pancakes and poured syrup on them.

"I don't think so," Callie said. "Her hair looked real nice—not like she had recently pulled a ski mask off it. And she'd been here long enough Bob had already served her a drink, since I wasn't here to do it." Bob was the owner and cook at The Check. He rarely left the kitchen.

"But we told you we suspected her the other day when we were here."

"No, you didn't. You talked about Aggie and Kimberly Banner, but you did not mention Jacqui."

I swallowed a forkful of pancake. "I guess we only talked about her to Jeff." I could have avoided the whole scene at The Blue Barn the night before if I'd told Callie we suspected Jacqui.

"Next time—though I hope there isn't a next time—tell me all your suspects. You know I know eighty-five percent of the stuff that happens in this town."

I nodded and took another bite. Then I hit my palm against my forehead. "I totally forgot to tell anyone what Marty said about Sam last night. I didn't even tell Darren. But if we know Jacqui wasn't involved, then I doubt Sam was, either."

"Maybe, maybe not. Tell us what he said," Aunt Star prompted.

I told them what Marty told me about the Dalrymple siblings. "And Veronica also mentioned his sister is on drugs. I didn't think anything of it at the time, so I didn't pass that info along to anyone either."

"You think she has long hair?" Aunt Star asked.

"The woman who was here with him did," Callie informed us. "Maybe that was his sister. She's a similar size to Jacqui."

The three of us looked at each other in silence.

"Did we just solve this robbery?" I asked.

"We may have," my aunt said. "You'd better tell Mitchell or Darren all this."

"Can I use your phone?" I asked Callie.

She nodded in the direction of the counter. "Go for it."

Mitchell hadn't returned to the station, so I filled Darren in.

"Don't you dare try to track these people down, Beckett."

"I won't. I'm leaving this one totally up to you."

"That's the response I was hoping to hear. I'd better go. Thanks for the info."

When I sat back down at the table, Callie gave me a sly smile, "I heard about the kiss Mitchell plastered on you at The Blue Barn the other night."

My face turned red.

She continued, "But I also know you eat lunch here with Marty every couple weeks. And you just mentioned talking to him last night. What's the deal there?"

The pancakes sat heavily in my stomach.

Aunt Star cut in, "They're just friends."

Callie glanced back and forth between the two of us with an incredulous look. "You sure *he* knows that?"

I nodded and pushed my half-empty plate away. Callie gave me a shrewd look but dropped the topic.

The bell over the diner door dinged, heralding the entrance of more customers. Callie said goodbye to us and headed to their table.

I looked at my watch. "I still have twenty minutes before work, which is enough time to go apologize to Jacqui."

"You are not going to Jacqui's house!" Aunt Star exclaimed.

"Why not? We know she wasn't involved. She's not going to hurt me. This is one conversation I'm not dreading today."

"Are you planning to tell her we think her boyfriend robbed her mother?"

"Absolutely not. Let me do this, please. I want to set things right with her, even if we're not exactly friends."

"Fine, but I'm going with you."

We bundled up once again and headed out. Aunt Star parked behind me on the street in front of Jacqui's house and followed me up the sidewalk.

I rang the doorbell, and then I stilled when I glanced through the triangle-shaped windows in the front door.

"You've got to be kidding me."

Chapter Twenty

"What?" Aunt Star peeked around me so she could see through the windows. "Oh, no."

A handsome yet scruffy-looking man wearing nothing but a worn pair of jeans stood inside. I had no doubt we were looking at Sam Dalrymple. While I considered our next move, the door wrenched open. Jacqui stood on the other side of the glass storm door in a set of skimpy pajamas. She gave us a fake smile, but her eyes betrayed her fear.

"Now's not a good time, ladies," she said loudly so we could hear through the glass. "Why don't you come back later? I'll call you."

She started to close the door, but after a split second of further deliberation, I opened the storm door and stepped inside. "What's going on here?"

Aunt Star grabbed my arm, but I shook her off. I wasn't leaving Jacqui alone with Sam. When I looked at him, I stilled again at the sight of the gun in his hands that wasn't visible before. I should've realized he might be armed.

He growled, "Get in here, both of you." He used the gun to wave us in.

Aunt Star followed me into the room, but I made sure to keep my body between her and Sam. He closed the door and motioned for us to all move to the couch. Aunt Star and I sat on either side of Jacqui, and I gripped her hand.

"What are you doing here?" she whispered.

"Where's Parker?" I whispered back.

"School, I hope. He spent the night with my mom."

I closed my eyes in relief that her nine-year-old son was not in the house.

"Shut up," Sam ordered. "What am I supposed to do with the three of you? Huh?"

I didn't know if that was a rhetorical question, or if he really wanted to know our thoughts, but I kept my mouth shut. He glared at each of us in turn, and I flinched when he waved the gun around.

"I don't think you intended to shoot Mr. Adamson," I blurted out.

Jacqui elbowed me in the side as Sam's gaze swung to mine. Thankfully the gun didn't swing with it.

"Beckett ..." my aunt warned under her breath.

"No, I want to hear what the lady has to say," Sam said.

"Sam, is it?" I asked.

He nodded.

I took a deep breath and pressed on. "You didn't want to shoot anybody. You only wanted to get in and out and escape with whatever money you could grab before the cops had time to arrive."

I didn't break eye contact with him as I continued, "You thought you'd have one or maybe two minutes to get the job done, but when you realized nobody could reach an alarm, you changed your plan. That's where you made your mistake. You were flying by the seat of your pants, the adrenaline was pumping, and when Perry slipped away to sound the alarm, you reacted on instinct." I was grasping at straws, but it made sense in my mind.

"How do you know all this?" He waved the gun some more, and Jacqui squeaked. "How do you know I didn't want to shoot that place up?"

I was beginning to sweat, still zipped up in my heavy coat, but I ignored the discomfort and answered his question. "First, you would have shot somebody immediately, if you were in the mood to shoot people. Second, I know you're a big deal in Taylorville. Best quarterback anybody in this area has ever seen. When you were younger, all the guys wanted to be you, and all the girls wanted to be with you." I was stretching the truth, but I figured it couldn't hurt to stroke the man's ego.

"You've been trying to recapture that feeling from high school ever since," I continued. "That's why you do the stuff you do now—so people won't forget you. You want a reputation, even if it's not the best one in the world. But killing somebody? No. That won't get you anything you want."

The gun slowly dropped to his side as he listened intently.

"You know what you should do now?" I asked. "Give yourself up. If what I just said is true, and I think it is, the best thing you can do for yourself and your reputation is to set the record straight. Don't let the people around here think you're a killer. You're not."

"I'm not."

"That's what I thought. Why'd you do it, though? Why did you rob the bank?"

"I did it partly for her." He pointed at Jacqui with his empty hand.

"Me?!" Jacqui exclaimed. "But why?"

"Because they wouldn't give you a job. I wanted to teach them a lesson. And I wanted you to know what I would do to stand up for you."

"But you robbed my mother!" Jacqui said. "And you shot her friend!"

"I didn't know your mom was going to be there, did I?"

He waved the gun, but not in our direction. I quickly thought back over the previous few minutes and realized he hadn't directly pointed the gun at any of us since Aunt Star and I walked in.

I stood. "There was no way you could have known," I reassured him.

Jacqui grabbed my arm to pull me back down, but I yanked it out of her grasp. The gun was fully down at Sam's side. I stepped toward him, and his hand jerked, but he didn't point the gun back up.

"Sam, give me the gun. You don't want to shoot me. You don't want to shoot any of us."

He lifted the gun toward me, and I sucked in a breath. One of the women behind me let out a strangled cry. Sam looked toward them and then released his grasp on the gun and let it dangle from his pointer finger. I carefully reached out to take it from him.

I had never handled a handgun before, but I gripped it in my hand and gently put my finger on the trigger. I kept it pointing away from all of us to keep from accidentally shooting anyone, though I tried to mentally prepare myself to shoot Sam in the lower body if necessary to protect my aunt and Jacqui.

"Sit on the loveseat behind you."

He obeyed.

"Aunt Star, call your boyfriend."

She stood, but before heading to the phone she grabbed a blanket off the back of the couch and draped it over Jacqui's shoulders. My aunt then shrugged out of her coat as she crossed the room to the phone.

"Her boyfriend?" Sam questioned me.

I unzipped my coat before I passed out from heatstroke.

"He's the Deputy Chief of Police."

Sam's eyes widened.

"And my boyfriend is a major crimes detective."

Sam dropped his head into his hands. "Man, am I glad I didn't shoot you."

While Sam wasn't looking, I removed my coat as quickly and carefully as I could while holding a loaded gun.

"Barbara, it's Starla," Aunt Star said into the phone. "I need to speak to Darren or Mitchell. It's urgent."

"How did this happen?" I asked Jacqui while Aunt Star was on hold.

Jacqui said, "When you told me what kind of car was seen speeding away from town, I realized it was the same type of car Sam's sister drives, and I started getting suspicious. I called him when I got home and asked him to come over so we could talk. Turns out we didn't take the time to chat until this morning."

I refrained from rolling my eyes.

"Babe," Aunt Star said into the phone, "I need you to come over to Jacqui Storm's house immediately. Bring your handcuffs." As if they weren't part of his uniform at all times. "And Mitchell. And maybe Frank and Jake. Whoever." Darren's voice increased in volume, but I couldn't make out his words. "We're safe," she said firmly. "Beckett has a gun, and she knows how to use it."

I wasn't sure I did, but I assumed she said it for Sam's sake.

"Just get over here." Aunt Star hung up before Darren could question her more. Then she returned to the couch and put an arm around Jacqui.

"So what happened this morning?" I asked from my position near Sam—but not near enough he could grab the gun again if he changed his mind about shooting us.

"We ate breakfast," Jacqui said, "and I finally got up the nerve to ask him if he knew anything about the robbery. Not fifteen seconds later, you showed up."

"Did you know he had a gun?" I asked her.

"I always carry a gun," Sam said.

"You shut your mouth," I said. "I'm not talking to you anymore. Maybe you didn't intend to shoot Perry, but you did shoot him. And you frightened both of our mothers," I pointed to Jacqui and then myself, "out of their wits."

He shot me a look of disbelief. "What does *your* mom have to do with it?"

I chose to answer his question even though I'd told him to be quiet. "She works at the bank."

Sam groaned and closed his eyes.

"You picked the wrong bank, dude." I narrowed my eyes at him. "By the way, you said you did this partly for Jacqui. Why else did you do it?"

I doubted he would answer, but he surprised me. "My sister owes somebody a lot of money. I figured why not kill two birds with one stone?"

Sirens sounded in the distance and consistently grew louder. Aunt Star crossed the room to open the door. Moments later, Darren and Mitchell rushed in with guns drawn, followed by Frank and Jake.

Mitchell took Sam's gun from my hand, dumped the bullets out onto the floor, and stuck it down the waistband of his pants. Then he wasn't sure where to train his own firearm. He settled on Sam, while Darren pointed his gun at Jacqui. Frank and Jake stood near the door with their weapons at the ready.

"Who are we arresting here?" Darren demanded.

"Just me." Sam sighed. "Jacqui knew nothing about it."

Darren looked at me, and I nodded in confirmation.

"He's telling the truth. And he didn't say so, but I'm almost certain his sister was the accomplice."

Darren turned his gun away from Jacqui and toward Sam, who held out his hands to be handcuffed.

"Nope." Mitchell quickly holstered his weapon and then grabbed Sam's wrists, pulled him to his feet, and spun him around in one swift movement. "Hands behind your back, buddy." He cuffed the man and pushed him across the room to Frank and Jake. "What's your sister's name?"

Sam didn't respond.

"Cora Westerly," Jacqui said.

"Take him to the station and put him in a holding cell until we feel like questioning him," Mitchell said to Frank. "Then go pick the sister up." He turned to Jacqui. "You know where she lives?"

"No, but she works at the dry cleaner in Taylorville. If she's not there, they'll know where she lives."

"Got it," Frank said. "We'll get her."

The moment Frank opened the storm door, Sam whined about the temperature, but Jake gave him a nudge onto the front porch.

"Let me put some clothes on, man!" Sam yelled. He wasn't even wearing shoes.

"You should have thought about that before you pulled a gun on three innocent women," Frank said before the door slammed behind them.

Jacqui burst into tears on Aunt Star's shoulder.

Meanwhile, Mitchell turned to me, crossed his arms over his chest, and gave me a piercing look. Darren looked at Aunt Star in much the same way.

I held my hands up. "We didn't come here to confront anyone. I promise. I thought we'd be perfectly safe. But to be fair, I did wait until you were back in town."

"Why did you come?" Jacqui asked between sniffles while Aunt Star patted her back.

"To apologize for suspecting you. Callie told us you were at The Check right after the robbery. I'm sorry I ever thought you could rob your own mother."

"Or an entire bank full of people I know?"

I dropped down on the couch and put an arm around her. "Or an entire bank full of people you know."

"I guess I should thank you for saving my life."

"He wasn't going to shoot you."

"You can't know that," Jacqui said.

"He never pointed the gun at any of us."

"He didn't?" Jacqui and Aunt Star asked in unison.

"No. I can pretty much guarantee Sam will never shoot anyone again. Once was enough."

"It'll be hard for him to get a gun in jail, which is where he'll be for a long time," Darren said. "To help make that happen, we'll need statements from all three of you."

"We'll come to the station," Aunt Star responded. "Give us a half hour to help Jacqui get ready."

She stood and pulled Jacqui up with her, and they disappeared down the hallway. Darren stepped outside, leaving Mitchell and me alone in the living room. Mitchell removed Sam's gun from his waistband and set it on a side table. Then he pulled me into his arms and squeezed me tightly.

"Mmph!" I said into his shoulder.

He loosened his hold on me. "Sorry."

I let myself relax against his body as he rubbed my back.

"You okay?"

"Mmhm."

"You're all sweaty."

I giggled at his unexpected statement. "You have a problem with my sweat?"

"Not at all. Just wondering why you're damp."

"I didn't get a chance to take my coat off until after I got the gun away from him."

"That's a part of this confrontation story I can't wait to hear."

I tipped my head back to look at him. "I truly didn't plan to confront anyone. I only wanted to make things right with Jacqui."

He chuckled and twirled a finger through one of my curls while still holding me close with his other hand. "That's one of the things I love about you."

My eyes widened at his use of the L-word.

"You wanted to make things right," his voice dropped to a whisper, "but you don't even like her."

"She's not so bad." I rested my cheek against his shoulder again. "I probably like her more than she likes me, considering I suspected her of robbing her own mother at gunpoint."

He let out a full laugh that vibrated all the way through me.

"Hey, look at me," he said.

I did.

"Are you nervous about that word I used a minute ago?"

I nodded. It was way too soon, especially considering the events of the previous days.

"There are many things I love about you. But I'm not ready to say the three big words yet, okay?"

I nodded again.

He added, "I know you want to take things slow, and we still have a lot to learn about each other."

I nodded one more time.

"Is there anything you want to tell me about yesterday?"

I didn't break eye contact with him. "I had a couple encounters that threw me for a loop, but I got it all worked out."

"You sure?"

I placed a hand over his heart and nodded. I knew I should tell him at least a little of what happened with Marty, but then the storm door creaked on its hinges, and we both turned toward it as Darren poked his head in.

"You coming?" Darren asked Mitchell.

Mitchell answered, "Give me thirty seconds to finish up here."

Darren nodded, and the door slammed shut.

"Only thirty?" I asked my one and only boyfriend.

"Let's make them count."

Chapter Twenty-One

I said a quick prayer before entering the hardware store.

"He's in his office," Todd informed me before I could ask.

I could feel him watching me as I climbed the stairs, and I kept my focus on the steps all the way up. When I reached the top, I turned and gave him a thumbs up. He laughed and returned the gesture.

Marty's office door was open halfway, so I knocked twice and pushed it fully open.

"Beckett." He dropped his pen, tipped back his chair, and perused me with a neutral expression.

I stood in the doorway and leaned against the frame for support. "Hi."

"You want to take a seat?" he asked cordially.

"No thanks." I didn't remove my coat.

He pressed his lips together. "Okay."

We gazed at each other for a moment. He knew what I had come to tell him, and he wasn't going to help me say it.

I twisted my hands together, much like I had the previous day. "I don't think we can be friends."

"It would probably not be a good idea to try."

"I'm sorry."

"Me, too." His face retained its blank expression.

A lump formed in my throat, and I looked down at my feet.

He said, "I heard you caught the bank robbers—well, one of them, at least."

My eyes returned to his face. "Yeah."

"Good job."

"Thanks."

He picked up his pen. "I need to finish these accounts."

"Right. See you later." I turned away from him.

"Bye, Beckett," he said so softly I almost didn't hear him.

My initial steps faltered, but I steeled myself and walked away. I knew I was making the right decision, no matter how much it hurt.

"What can I do for you?" Edna Thorn asked me from across her desk at *The Cherry Hill Standard* newspaper office.

I opened my mouth but then closed it again.

"Spit it out. I have a thousand things to do."

"You know how you saw me with Marty James the other day?"

"Do you mean the other *days?*"

"Yes." My cheeks turned pink.

She raised an eyebrow.

"I want you to know we're not together," I said.

"Because you're dating the detective?"

I nodded.

"Does he know about Marty?" she asked.

"There's nothing to know about Marty."

She tapped a fingernail on her desk. "So you ended things with him?"

"There was nothing to end." Except a friendship.

"I think you may be deluded. I have eyes and a brain. The man is in love with you."

I groaned. "Here's the deal. I didn't know he was interested in me." I held a hand up when she started to speak. "That's an ongoing problem with me, I've been told. I thought we were just friends. But when I found out he wanted more, I told him I'm dating Mitchell, which essentially ended our friendship. I'm only telling you about this because of what you saw. I don't want you to think I'm dating two men at once. That's not my style."

"I didn't think it was."

"So if you talk to Mitchell—Detective Crowe—I'd appreciate you not saying anything about what you saw."

"I hadn't planned on it. He won't hear it from me. But if you think he's not going to find out about your friendship or whatever it was with Marty, I think you're wrong. You need to tell him before he hears it from somebody else. I'm not the only person who saw you together outside the bank, and though I was the only customer at the hardware store, Todd was there, too."

"Tell us what happened," Veronica said to me. "I can't believe I missed it."

"Honey ..." Pastor Coker's voice sounded pained.

"I know, I know." Veronica patted her husband's hand. "You're glad I did."

The three of us were eating lunch at their kitchen table. I had called from Jacqui's that morning to tell them why I would be late for work. Pastor Coker told me to take the day off, but Veronica demanded I join them for a late lunch.

I filled them in on the bank-robbery-related events of the

previous twenty hours, leaving out the private details about Aggie. I was determined to let her share her story when and how she chose to. Veronica asked me numerous questions as I spoke, but Pastor Coker listened silently.

The second her husband finished his pie, Veronica said to him, "Isn't it about time for you to head back over to the church?"

He looked back and forth between his wife and me, wiped his mouth, and pushed up from the table. "Somebody has to keep things running. I'm just glad I don't need to type up the bulletin. The good Lord knew you needed to get that done yesterday, my dear."

"Indeed, he did," I replied.

"Bye, Harold," Veronica said pointedly.

He said goodbye and left through the back door.

"Now," Veronica said, "tell me everything else."

An hour later, Veronica and I stood outside Aggie's door. I announced myself as I knocked, to help calm her fears. Aggie opened the door with an expectant look, but her expression turned guarded when she spotted Veronica behind me.

"This is Veronica Coker." I pulled her around to my side. "She's the pastor's wife at First Community Church, where I work. And she's a very good friend. She gives excellent advice and knows how to keep a secret. I thought you two would enjoy getting to know each other." It had actually been Veronica's idea, but I was fully on board.

"Nice to meet you." Aggie gave us a shy smile and invited us into her tiny living room.

Veronica and I sat on the love seat, and Aggie dragged a wooden chair over from beside the door and sat across from us. Then she popped back up. "Where are my manners? Would you like something to drink?"

"No, child," Veronica said. "We just ate lunch. Take a seat and tell us all about yourself—as much as you feel comfortable with."

Aggie looked at me. "Did Officer Turley tell you everything?"

I nodded. "But I haven't told Mrs. Coker anything. I haven't told anyone anything. I didn't know how much you'd want me to tell."

"Thank you."

"I also want to apologize for suspecting you. I am so sorry, and I hope you can forgive me."

"I do. I completely understand why you thought that. You weren't wrong that there was something strange going on with me."

"I'm glad we know the truth now, so you don't have to hide your true self anymore. You know they caught the robbers, right?" I asked her.

"Detective Crowe called to tell me. I'm so relieved."

"We all are, but maybe not as much as you."

She nodded, and then she told us everything.

Veronica held her as she cried.

My mother insisted on inviting a crowd to dinner to celebrate solving the case. We couldn't all fit at the kitchen table, so my parents, the Cokers, Suzanne, and Jacqui's son Parker ate at the table while the rest of us congregated in the living room with our plates of lasagna. Jeff and Jacqui took my parents' chairs, I shared the couch with Mitchell and Aggie, and Darren and Aunt Star sat on the floor in front of the TV.

Aggie had told Veronica and me she was going to continue to go by Aggie, while retaining Margaret Silverton as her legal name. Though she knew word would soon get out about her past, she didn't want to confuse people in town by changing her first name again, and the new nickname also symbolized her fresh start.

She had asked me to relay the basic details of her story to anyone who would be at dinner who didn't already know, so she wouldn't be expected to either keep up the pretense or explain the situation in front of a large crowd. I had invited Jacqui and Suzanne to come to my parents' a half hour early to take care of it.

"Aggie," Jacqui said, and I braced myself for what she might say. "Tell us your favorite thing about living in Cherry Hill."

"All of you," Aggie replied without hesitation, "and everyone else at the bank. You've all been so kind." Tears glistened in her eyes, and I reached over to hold her hand. "Even after knowing I lied to you. I'm so sorry."

"No," Jeff said, "we're sorry for what you've been through."

I squeezed Aggie's hand as I gave Jeff a speculative look. Now that he knew the truth about Aggie, I wondered if he might be interested in her. Sure, he had suspected her of armed robbery, but hadn't I suspected Marty of murder? My chest constricted at the thought of Marty.

"Thank you," Aggie whispered.

I figured she couldn't deal with any more tears, and I needed to stop thinking about Marty, so I told her a story about something ridiculous Jeff did in high school. Throughout the rest of the meal, we regaled Aggie and Mitchell with stories of our Cherry Hill youth.

After dessert, Darren and Mitchell announced they needed to head back to the police station for a few more hours. They said their goodbyes, and Mitchell asked me to walk him to his truck.

I pulled on my coat and gloves and headed out the door hand in hand with him. When we reached the pickup, he leaned back against the driver's door and pulled me against him.

"It's like the Arctic tundra out here, so I won't keep you long," he said.

"I don't mind." I had changed out of my dress and into jeans and a sweater before dinner.

"I think you do, but I know what you're saying." He gave me a quick kiss. "You were amazing in there."

My forehead wrinkled. "What do you mean?"

"You knew exactly how to make Aggie feel comfortable— like she belongs. You're so good at that." He placed a hand on the side of my face and swept his thumb across my cheek, and I pressed into the warmth of his touch. I thought it was ridiculous he wasn't wearing gloves, but I was thankful for it in the moment.

"Thank you for saying that. I did think she might be a bank robber, though, so I'm not all that fantastic."

"You might lose a few points for that," he admitted. "But you gained a whole lot more by understanding her situation and bringing her into your world."

"It's not about points."

"I know it's not, which is another thing I love about you."

Heat crept up my neck, despite the sub-freezing temperature.

"And there's another." He pressed his lips to my neck, which would have given me goosebumps if I didn't already have them.

"You know what I *don't* love about you?" I asked.

He kissed the tip of my nearly frozen nose. "What?"

"The way you've made it your mission in life to make me blush as often as possible."

"It's one of my favorite things in the world." He rested his forehead against mine.

"Why?"

"Because you're absolutely adorable when you blush."

"I am not! The red clashes with my hair."

"I disagree." He attempted to run his fingers through the curls in question, but they got stuck.

I giggled as I helped him get untangled. "Too much Aqua Net, I guess."

"It doesn't help that my fingers are half numb."

I unzipped my coat and pulled his arms around me underneath it. He drew me tightly against him so my front wouldn't get cold.

"Why do you refuse to tell me when you're uncomfortable?" I asked.

"Because life's not about my comfort."

"Oh yeah, that's right. It's about mine." I smirked at him.

"You'd better believe it, baby."

I laughed, but my smile faded when I realized we needed to have a conversation that might make both of us uncomfortable.

"Where'd your smile go?"

"There's something I need to talk to you about."

"About yesterday?"

I nodded.

"Hold that thought. Let's get in the truck. Something tells me I might need the comfort of the heater for this."

He opened the door and before I could climb in, he scooped me up and set me in the driver's seat. I slid over, and he hopped in and started the engine. Then he angled himself toward me and put his hands in his jacket pockets.

"You know Marty James?" I asked.

"I do."

"Yesterday I found out he wants to date me."

Mitchell's jaw tensed. "How did you find that out?"

"After the bank robbery, Aunt Star told me she suspected he might be interested in me. Then yesterday, I tripped and fell in the hardware store, and he helped me up, and then he ...," I trailed off.

"He what?" Mitchell's tone was even, but his eyes were sharp.

I turned my head away from him. "He hugged me." I closed my eyes. "And I hugged him back."

He let out a breath. "You're a hugger. I don't care if you hug people. What made this hug so different you can't look me in the eye?"

How could I explain what happened without going into detail? "The way he ... I ...," I sighed. "I could tell he had feelings for me beyond friendship."

"Okay."

"I told him he and I are only friends, and I'm dating you."

"He didn't know about me?"

I turned back to him. "How would he? Nobody outside my family and closest friends knew about us until you arrived at the bar Tuesday night."

"True."

"Are you mad?" I bit my lip and looked out the window instead of at him.

"Should I be?"

I shrugged. "After our conversation about Jeff, I thought you might be, whether you should or not." I shot him a glance. "Marty knows me pretty well—much better than Jeff does."

"Not well enough to know about me, though."

"No."

"Listen," he turned my face toward his, "I've been thinking

about what you said the other night, and you're right. It's unfair for me to get upset that you have a history—even if only a friendship—with other men in your life. I don't want you to feel like you need to hide that from me. And I'll do my best not to feel jealous of those other guys."

"If you are jealous, though, I want to know," I said. "I don't want you to hide that from me, either."

He nodded and took a deep breath. "The bottom line here is you didn't know Marty wanted more than friendship, and he didn't know about me. Neither of you did anything wrong, based on the knowledge you had at the time, so there's no reason for me to be mad. But I'm confused by why you're so upset about it."

"Because it was all my fault it happened. I should have been able to tell how he felt before he acted on it. Then I could have told him you and I are together, which would have kept him from feeling like a fool, and we might still be friends. I felt so bad about the whole thing. I still do."

He took my gloved hands in his. "And there's yet another example of how much you care about other people."

I shook my head, pulled my hands away, and stared out the windshield. "No. There's nothing good about what happened. I lost a friendship over my ignorance." My throat began to close up.

"He doesn't want to be your friend anymore?"

"No," I choked out.

"I get that. I wouldn't want to only be friends with you, either. But if losing his friendship makes you sad, that makes me sad."

He wrapped an arm around me, pulled me tightly against his side, and kissed my temple. I rested my head on his shoulder and relaxed into him. I didn't want to leave him, but he needed to get back to the police station.

Thinking about the case reminded me of something. "You realize I'm a witness again, right?"

"I am well aware. But I'm not letting that stop us anymore."

A smile spread across my face. "Really?"

"Definitely." He tilted my face toward his. "I'm not putting us on hold any longer, especially considering your current popularity with the single men of Cherry Hill. Now, is there anything else you need to tell me?"

I shook my head.

"Good." He trailed a thumb across my thawing lips. "Then how about we warm these up?"

My body tingled all the way down to my toes. "Yes, please."

Continue the Series!

Available at Amazon.com and
other online retailers

Have you read the first two Totally 80s Mysteries?

Available at Amazon.com and other online retailers

Mystery Journals

Do you want an easy way to keep track of all the suspects or other characters in mysteries? These journals allow mystery readers to record suspects, other characters, motives, means, opportunity, and more!

Available at Amazon.com

Throwback RomComs

Author Dana Wilkerson also writes romcoms set in Chicago in the late 1980s! These books are loosely connected to the Totally 80s Mysteries and feature some of Beckett's cousins and their friends.

Available at Amazon.com

About the Author

D.A. (Dana) Wilkerson is the author of the Totally 80s Mysteries cozy mystery series and the Throwback Romcoms series (as Dana Wilkerson). She has been a professional writer and editor for almost two decades and was the collaborative writer of two non-fiction *New York Times* best sellers: *The Vow: The True Events That Inspired the Movie* (Kim and Krickitt Carpenter) and *Balancing It All* (Candace Cameron Bure).

Dana lives in Oklahoma and enjoys traveling, reading, being an aunt, binge-watching crime shows, and attending Oklahoma City Thunder basketball games.

danawilkerson.com

If you enjoyed this book, join author D.A. Wilkerson's mailing list!

When you join the list, you don't just receive a few emails a month. You get book and music playlist recommendations, 1980s nostalgia, writing updates, sneak peeks of upcoming books, subscriber-only freebies and discounts, and more. Come join the fun!

To join, go to danawilkerson.com and click "Sign Up."